YOU CAN'T SCARE ME!

Look for more Goosebumps books
by R.L. Stine:

Goosebumps

YOU CAN'T SCARE ME!

R.L. STINE

AN
APPLE
PAPERBACK

SCHOLASTIC INC.
New York Toronto London Auckland Sydney

No part of this publication may be reproduced in whole or in part, or stored in a retrieval system, or transmitted in any form or by any means, electronic, mechanical, photocopying, recording, or otherwise, without written permission of the publisher. For information regarding permission, write to Scholastic Inc., 730 Broadway, New York, NY 10003.

ISBN 0-590-49450-3

24 23 22 21 20   6 7 8 9/9

Printed in the U.S.A.   40

First Scholastic printing, January 1994

1

The day we decided to scare Courtney was the day of our class field trip.

Mr. Melvin, our teacher, and Ms. Prince, the other sixth-grade teacher, stood counting us as we boarded the yellow school bus.

Courtney was first in line, of course. Courtney makes sure she is always first in line. Her friend Denise boarded right behind her.

It was a gray day. Dark storm clouds rolled overhead, blocking the sun. The guy on the radio said there was a ninety percent chance of rain.

I didn't care. I was happy to be getting out of school.

I pushed my friend Hat into the kid in front of him. His real name is Herbie, but everyone calls him Hat. That's because no one has ever seen him without a baseball cap on his head. I've known Hat since fourth grade, and I don't think I've ever seen his hair.

The kid in front spun around and shoved Hat back at me.

"Hey — give me a break!" Hat shouted. He slugged me hard on the shoulder. "You made me swallow my gum, Eddie."

"Hey, guys, be cool," Mr. Melvin said, frowning at us. He's the kind of teacher who always says things like "be cool" and tries to act like he's our friend. But he's a pretty good teacher, anyway.

And he takes us on a lot of field trips, which *is* cool.

"Why are we going to a forest?" Hat grumbled, slipping another piece of bubble gum into his mouth. "What are we supposed to look for?"

"Trees, I guess," I replied. I didn't remember why we were going to Greene Forest. I just remembered we were supposed to take notes.

"Eddie, want some bubble gum?"

I turned around to see my friend Charlene right behind me in line. She and my other friend Molly had big gobs of grape gum in their mouths and were chewing hard.

"Molly, how can you chew that stuff with braces?" I asked.

She opened her mouth in a wide grin, showing me her teeth. "It doesn't stick too much," she said.

Molly's braces are red and blue. She's always showing them off. I don't know why.

Molly and Charlene look so much alike, almost like sisters. They both have short brown hair and brown eyes. They're both about my height, five two. They both wear faded jeans and big, oversized T-shirts all the time. The only difference between Molly and Charlene is that Molly wears glasses and has braces, and Charlene doesn't.

"I'll protect you two in the deep, dark forest," I teased. "You know. In case you're attacked by fleas or something."

"Eddie's a real macho guy," Hat said, grinning. "He's real brave." He punched my shoulder. Hard.

I pretended it didn't hurt.

"You both have fleas," Charlene said.

"We'll protect *you*, Eddie," Molly offered. "There might be some vicious worms there!"

Hat, Molly, and Charlene burst out laughing. Molly was teasing me about the time the four of us went fishing at Muddy Creek, and I had a little trouble putting a worm on my hook.

"I wasn't afraid of that worm!" I cried angrily. "It was just yucky, that's all."

I scowled at Molly, but I wasn't really angry. I'm used to being teased. Kids always make fun of my freckles and my red hair. And my older brother, Kevin, calls me Bugs. He says I look just like Bugs Bunny because my two front teeth stick out.

"What's up, doc? What's up, doc?" That's all Kevin ever says to me. He and his high school pals think it's a riot.

I climbed onto the bus and scrambled past Hat to get a window seat. Courtney and Denise had taken the front seat, of course. Courtney was brushing her long, blonde hair, using the bus window as a mirror. Denise was writing something in her notebook.

Hat slammed into me, and I stumbled down the aisle. He quickly slid into the seat and moved to the window. "Hey — no fair!" I shouted.

He giggled his high-pitched giggle and grinned at me. Hat is my best pal, but I have to admit he's sort of goofy-looking. I mean, he's always grinning, sort of like Dopey in *Snow White and the Seven Dwarfs*. And he has really big ears that bend down beneath his baseball cap, sort of doubled over.

He's a good guy. He really makes Molly, Charlene, and me laugh all the time.

"I get the window going back," I said, slumping down beside Hat. Charlene messed up my hair as she walked past.

"Why do they call it Greene Forest?" Hat asked, pressing his nose against the window, watching it steam up from his breath. "Why not Blue Forest or Red Forest?"

"A guy named Greene used to own it," I told him. "He gave the land to the city when he died."

"I knew that," Hat said. What a liar.

I spun his cap around till it was backwards. He really hates that. But he deserved it for grabbing the window seat.

A few minutes later, the bus was bouncing toward Greene Forest. A few minutes after that, we were piling out of the bus, staring at the tall trees that reached up to the dark, cloudy sky.

"Make two columns on your work sheet," Ms. Prince was telling everyone. "One for wildlife and one for plantlife."

"I'm putting *you* down as plantlife," I told Charlene.

She stuck her tongue out at me with the big, purple blob of bubble gum on the tip. Hat slapped her on the back really hard, and the wad of bubble gum went flying.

Charlene cried out angrily and tried to slug him, but Hat backed away to safety. He was too fast for her.

The teachers divided us into groups, and we began to explore the forest. We followed a narrow dirt path that twisted through the trees.

It was cooler in the forest, and dark. I wished the sun would come out.

"What's that green stuff on that tree?" Hat asked me, pointing. "Is that moss? Is moss wildlife or plantlife?"

"You should know," I told him. "You have it growing on your back!"

Molly and Charlene laughed, but Hat didn't. "Can't you ever be serious?" He scribbled something on his work sheet.

I glanced down at mine. I hadn't written anything yet. I mean, I'd only seen a bunch of trees and some weeds. Who cared about writing *that* down?

"The creatures are hiding," Ms. Prince was telling the group of kids ahead of us. "Search for their hiding places. Look for holes in the ground and in trees. Look for hidden nests."

I gazed up at the trees above my head. The leaves were too thick to see any nests. I was about to tell Hat he should look under some rocks because that's where he came from. But before I could, I heard a hushed cry behind us.

"Ssshhh! Look! A deer!"

We all turned back to see who had called out. Of course it was Courtney. Who *else* would be the first to spot a deer?

She and Denise were frozen like statues, staring into a narrow space between the trees. Courtney kept raising her finger to her lips, signaling for everyone to be silent.

Hat, Molly, Charlene, and I went running over to see the deer. "I don't see anything," I said, squinting hard into the trees.

"It ran away," Courtney told me.

"You missed it," Denise added. I watched her write *deer* on her work sheet under wildlife. She already had four other creatures on her list. I didn't have any.

"Did you see the sleeping bat?" Courtney asked me.

"Bat?" I don't like bats. They're so ugly. And what if one bites you?

"It was hanging on that tree," Courtney said, pointing behind us. "How could you miss it?"

I shrugged.

"There's a birch tree," Denise told Courtney. "And there's a weeping beech tree. Add them to the list."

Hat, Molly, and Charlene had moved on along the trail, and I hurried to catch up to them. Courtney and Denise were working too hard, in my opinion. Field trips are supposed to be for goofing and having fun away from school.

We made our way slowly through the forest. After a while, the sun came out and sent shafts of yellow light down through the trees.

I tried to push Hat into a huge patch of poison ivy. But he dodged away from me, and I went sprawling face down in the dirt.

I was still brushing myself off when I saw the snake.

Right beside my left sneaker.

It was bright green, and big.

I stopped breathing. I stared down at it.

I had nearly stepped on it.

As I stared helplessly, it arched its head, opened its jaws, and darted forward to bite my leg.

I opened my mouth to scream, but no sound came out.

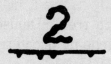

The snake dived toward me. I shut my eyes and waited for the stab of pain.

"Ohh." A low, frightened cry escaped my lips.

I opened my eyes to see Courtney holding up the snake. "Courtney — I — I — " I stammered.

"Eddie, you're not scared of *this*, are you?" Courtney demanded, raising the snake to my face. Its black eyes stared up at me. It flicked its tongue.

"It's a harmless green snake, Eddie," Courtney said. "You *can't* be afraid of a green snake!"

I heard Denise snickering behind me.

Courtney petted the snake, stroking it, letting it slide through her fingers.

"Uh . . . I wasn't really scared," I muttered. But my voice trembled. I could tell Courtney didn't believe me.

"A harmless green snake," she repeated. She set the snake down on the ground.

I jumped back. I thought it was coming for me again.

8

But it slid silently into the weeds.

Hat laughed. A high-pitched, nervous laugh.

Denise shook her head scornfully.

"Add that to the list," Courtney told her. "Green snake. That makes seven in the wildlife column."

"We should write down *chicken*," Denise said, staring at me. "That would make eight."

"Cluck cluck," I replied bitterly. I motioned for my friends to follow me, and we hurried up the path. We could hear Courtney and Denise both laughing.

"Don't feel bad," Hat said to me, patting my shoulder. "Just because she made you look like a total jerk."

Molly laughed, but Charlene didn't. "Courtney was just showing off," Charlene said to me. "For a change."

"I wish that snake had bitten her perfect nose," Molly added. "You know. Put a little dent in it."

"I really wasn't afraid," I insisted shrilly. "The snake surprised me, that's all. I knew it was harmless."

"Yeah. Right," Hat replied, rolling his beady little black eyes. I made a swipe at his cap but missed.

"Coming through! Coming through!" Courtney called. She and Denise hurried past us, swinging their work sheets in one hand as they passed by.

Denise turned and hissed at me like a snake. Courtney laughed.

"I suppose they'll be teasing me about the green snake for the next hundred years," I said with a sigh.

"We'll *all* tease you about it for a hundred years," Molly promised.

I trudged unhappily along the path. Golden sunshine filtered down through the trees, but it didn't brighten my spirits. A cute red-furred squirrel scampered across the path. I wasn't interested.

My day had been ruined.

Ruined by Courtney and that stupid green snake.

I could hear kids up ahead laughing about it. Every time I looked at Hat, he grinned at me as if to say, "You really blew it today, Eddie."

It's not a big deal, I kept telling myself. So I got scared of a snake. And I had to be rescued by Courtney. So what?

"Look out, Eddie. There's a caterpillar. It might bite!" some kid called from a clump of tall weeds up ahead.

"Give me a break!" I cried angrily.

As I made my way along the path, the forest became a bright green blur to me. Other kids were busy adding to the lists on their work sheets.

But I couldn't see anything to add. The air became hot and damp. My T-shirt stuck to my back. Little white gnats flew around my face.

I was really glad when the path ended and we stepped out near the parking lot. We had made a complete circle. The school bus stood at the edge of the grass, its door open invitingly.

But no one was getting on the bus.

To my surprise, I saw a big crowd of kids huddled in a circle several feet from the bus. They were standing silently, staring straight ahead.

"What — what's up?" I called to Charlene, who was hurrying toward the silent circle of kids.

"It's Courtney!" she called back.

I began running, too.

The kids were huddled so silently. No one moved.

Had something terrible happened to Courtney?

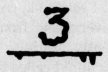

3

What happened to her? Did she faint or something? Was she bitten by some kind of forest
animal?

I ran across the grass and pushed my way into
the circle of kids.

And I saw Courtney standing in the center of
the circle, an excited smile on her face.

I was wrong. Nothing terrible had happened to
Courtney.

She was showing off again.

She had her hand raised and was showing
everyone her open palm. Two enormous bumble-
bees were in her hand, walking across her palm.

I sucked in my breath and stared along with
the others.

Courtney's smile grew wider as her eyes landed
on me.

One of the bees had crossed her wrist and was
walking down her arm. The other bee stood in the
center of her palm.

Mr. Melvin and Ms. Prince stood in the circle across from Courtney. They had admiring expressions on their faces. Mr. Melvin was smiling. Ms. Prince had her arms crossed tensely in front of her. She looked a little more worried than Mr. Melvin.

"Bees will not sting you unless they are provoked," Courtney said softly.

"What do they feel like?" a kid asked.

"They kind of tickle," Courtney told him.

Some kids hid their eyes. A few others groaned or shuddered.

"Get *rid* of them!" someone urged.

The bee crawled up Courtney's arm toward the sleeve of her T-shirt. I wondered what she'd do if it crawled under her shirt.

Would she panic then?

Would she go totally nuts, screaming and thrashing her arms, trying to get it out?

No. No way. Not Courtney.

Cool, calm Courtney would never panic.

The other bee walked slowly across her hand.

"It tickles. It really does," Courtney giggled. Her blonde hair gleamed in the sunlight. Her blue eyes twinkled excitedly.

Come on, bee — sting! STING! I urged silently.

I wondered if anyone else had the same secret wish.

It was a mean thought, I admit. But Courtney was really asking for it.

Come on — just one little sting! I begged, concentrating with all my might.

The bee on her arm turned around when it reached the T-shirt sleeve and made its way back slowly toward Courtney's elbow.

"Bees are really very gentle," Courtney said softly.

Both bees were in her palm now.

Courtney smiled at me. I felt a shiver go down my back. How does she *do* that? I wondered.

I had to admit to myself that I was afraid of bees. I'd always been afraid of them, ever since I'd been stung when I was a little kid.

"Would anyone else like to try this?" Courtney asked.

Nervous laughter rose up from the circle. No one was crazy enough to volunteer.

"Here, Eddie — catch!" Courtney cried.

And before I could move or shout or duck or do *anything* — she pulled back her hand and tossed both bees at me!

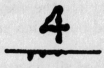

4

I screamed and stepped back.

I heard loud gasps all around.

One of the bees hit my shoulder and dropped to the grass.

The other bee fluttered onto the front of Hat's shirt and stuck there.

"Get it off! Get it off!" Hat screamed. He shook his shirt with both hands and did a wild, frightened dance.

Some kids were screaming. But most everyone was laughing uproariously.

I had my eye on the bee on the grass. It buzzed loudly off the ground and made a dive for my face.

"Whoa!" I screamed and dropped to my knees, flailing my hands above my head.

"I think it's time to get back to school," I heard Mr. Melvin say over the laughter of the other kids.

Courtney flashed me a smug grin as I walked past her down the aisle on the bus. I kept my eyes straight ahead and walked faster, ignoring her.

Some kids were making buzzing bee sounds. Others were hissing like snakes. Everyone thought it was a total riot that Hat and I had acted like such chickens.

I slumped down into the very last seat with a sigh. Hat dropped beside me and pulled his cap down over his eyes.

The seat stretched all the way across the back of the bus. Molly and Charlene joined us. Charlene was chewing her bubble gum furiously. Molly was trying to unstick her gum from her braces.

None of us said a word until the bus pulled away.

Then we started to grumble in low voices about Courtney and what a show-off she was. "She just thinks she's the greatest," Hat muttered unhappily.

"She acts as if she isn't afraid of anything," Charlene said. "Like she's Superwoman or something."

"Throwing those bees at Eddie was a mean joke," Molly added, still struggling to unstick the gum from her braces.

"She knows what a chicken Eddie is," Hat said. "She knew he'd scream and carry on like a jerk."

"Well, so did you!" I cried, not meaning to sound so babyish.

"Hey, I'm on *your* side!" Hat insisted, giving me a shove.

I shoved him back. I was really angry. Mostly with myself, I guess.

"There's got to be *something* that Courtney is afraid of," Charlene said thoughtfully.

The bus stopped at a red light. I glanced out the window and saw that we were at the woods that led to Muddy Creek. "Maybe she's afraid of the Mud Monsters," I suggested.

My three friends laughed bitterly. "No way," Charlene said. "No one really believes in the Mud Monsters anymore. That's a stupid old fairy tale. No way Courtney would be afraid of them."

There's a legend in our town that the Mud Monsters live under the muddy banks of the creek. And sometimes when the moon is full, the Mud Monsters rise up from the creek bed, all dripping with mud, and look for victims to pull down in the mud with them.

It's a good story. I used to believe it when I was a little kid. My brother, Kevin, always took me into the woods there. He would tell me about the Mud Monsters rising up. Then he'd start to point and tremble and say that he saw them. I tried not to get scared. But I couldn't help it. I always started screaming and running for my life!

"Is your brother still making that movie about the Mud Monsters?" Hat asked.

I nodded. "Yeah. You should see the disgusting costumes he and his friends cooked up. They're really gross."

Kevin and some of his friends were making a home video for one of their high school courses. It was a horror movie called *The Mud Monsters of Muddy Creek*.

I begged him to let me be in it. But he said he couldn't take the risk. "What if the *real* Mud Monsters rose up and came after you?" he asked, grinning at me.

I tried to explain that I was too old, that he couldn't scare me with that stuff anymore. But Kevin still wouldn't let me be in the video.

The bus started with a jolt. I glanced up to the front and saw Courtney and Denise staring back at me, laughing.

I turned to my friends. "We've got to find a way to scare Courtney," I said heatedly. "We've *got* to!"

"Eddie's right," Hat quickly agreed. "We've got to find a way to scare Courtney and embarrass her in front of a whole bunch of kids. Otherwise, she'll never let us forget today."

"But she's so brave, so totally fearless," Charlene said, shaking her head. "What could we possibly do to frighten her?"

We all moaned quietly, shaking our heads, thinking hard.

Then I saw an evil smile break across Molly's face. She pushed her glasses up on her nose. Behind them, her brown eyes sparkled with excitement. "I think I have an idea," she whispered.

5

"My brother has a disgusting rubber snake," Molly whispered. Her excited grin grew wider.

The four of us huddled together on the edge of the back seat. Every time the bus bounced, we nearly fell to the floor.

"Courtney isn't afraid of snakes," Hat interrupted. "She likes to pet them. Remember?"

"That was a stupid green snake," Molly whispered. "My brother's rubber snake is big and black. The mouth is open. It's got these huge, pointy white fangs. It's got a fierce expression on its face, and — "

"Does it look real or does it look fake?" I asked.

The bus hit a hard bump. We all bounced a foot straight up.

"It looks real," Molly replied, her eyes flashing behind her glasses. "And it feels warm and kind of sticky."

"Yuck!" Charlene exclaimed, making a face.

"He's scared me with it a dozen times," Molly confessed. "It's so real and disgusting, I'm fooled by it every time. Once when I reached under my pillow in the middle of the night and felt it there, I screamed for at least an hour. No one could get me to stop."

"Great!" Hat declared.

I still had my doubts. "You really think it'll make Courtney scream?"

Molly nodded. "She'll freak. She'll totally freak. This rubber snake is ugly enough to scare a *real* snake!"

We all laughed loudly. Some kids in the front turned to see what was so funny. I could see Courtney and Denise in the front seat, writing in their notebooks. They were probably copying their work sheet lists over. They both *had* to be perfect students in every way.

"I can't wait to scare Courtney," I said as the bus pulled up to our school. "You sure you can get this snake from your brother, Molly?"

Molly grinned at me. "I know which drawer he keeps it in. I'll just borrow it."

"But what are we going to do with it?" Charlene demanded. "How are we going to scare Courtney with it? Where are we going to hide it?"

"In her lunch bag, of course," Molly replied.

The four of us climbed off the bus with big smiles on our faces.

* * *

The lunch bags were kept on a low bookshelf in the back of our classroom. My class always eats lunch right in our classroom. Our school is very small so a cafeteria was never built. Courtney's lunch was always easy to spot. It was the biggest one on the shelf.

Her mother always packed her *two* sandwiches and *two* boxes of juice. Plus a bag of potato chips and an apple, some string cheese, and usually a fruit rollup or two.

I don't know why Courtney's mom gave her such big lunches. There was no way Courtney could eat it all. She became a big hero at lunchtime because she shared a lot of it with kids who had crummy lunches.

The next morning, I got to school a little late. The lunch bags were already spread out on the low shelf. I could see Courtney's overstuffed brown paper bag at the end.

I studied Courtney's lunch bag as I set mine down at the other end. Had Molly succeeded in her mission? Had she stuffed the rubber snake into the bag?

I couldn't tell by looking at the bag. But I *could* tell by looking at Molly. Her face was bright red, and she kept darting nervous glances at me.

Yes.

Molly had succeeded.

Now we just had to survive the three and a half hours until lunchtime.

21

How would I be able to concentrate on anything? I kept turning around in my seat and glancing back at Courtney's bulging lunch bag.

I kept imagining what was about to happen. I pictured the wonderful scene again and again. I saw Courtney sitting across the table from Denise, as she always did. I saw her chattering away. I saw her reach into the brown paper bag. . . .

I saw the horrified look on Courtney's face. I imagined her scream. I imagined the snake popping up from the bag, its fangs bared, its eyes glowing like hot coals.

I pictured Courtney shrieking in fright and everyone else laughing at her, making fun of her. I imagined myself walking over casually and picking up the snake. "Why, it's only rubber, Courtney," I'd say, holding it up high so everyone could see. "You shouldn't be afraid of rubber snakes. They're harmless. Perfectly harmless!"

What a victory!

All morning long, Hat, Molly, Charlene, and I kept grinning at each other, casting secret glances back and forth. I don't think we heard a single word Mr. Melvin said.

I couldn't tell you what spelling words were written on the blackboard. And I couldn't tell you what kind of math was on my review sheet. It was just a blur of numbers and squiggly signs to me.

My three friends and I spent most of the morning staring eagerly at the clock. Finally, lunchtime rolled around.

We hung back, all four of us. We waited at our tables and watched Courtney and Denise walk together to the back of the room to get their lunches.

We watched Courtney bend down in front of the bookshelf. First she handed Denise's lunch up to her. Then she picked up her own bag.

The two of them made their way to the table where they always sat. They pulled out chairs and sat down across from each other.

This is it, I thought, holding my breath.

This is the big moment.

My friends and I hurried to get our lunches. We didn't want anyone to wonder why we were just standing there staring at Courtney.

We sat down at our usual table. I kept my eyes glued on Courtney. I was so nervous and eager, I thought I would burst!

Courtney started to open her lunch bag.

Just then, everyone heard a low groan from the back of the room. It was Mr. Melvin. "Oh, no," he cried. "I forgot my lunch today."

"That's no problem," Courtney called back to him.

Mr. Melvin walked over to her table. He leaned down and started talking to her. I couldn't hear what they were saying. It's always really noisy in the room at lunchtime with everyone talking and laughing and crinkling their lunch bags and unwrapping their food.

Hat, Molly, Charlene, and I were the only ones in the room who were being quiet. We watched as Courtney and Mr. Melvin continued to talk.

"What are they talking about?" Hat whispered to me. "Why doesn't he let her open her bag?"

I shrugged, keeping my eyes on Courtney. She had a thoughtful expression on her face. Then she smiled up at him.

Then she handed him her lunch bag.

"No, really, it's fine," Courtney said to Mr. Melvin. "You can have some of my lunch. You know my mom always packs too much."

"Oh, no," I groaned. I suddenly felt sick.

"Should we warn him?" Hat asked me.

Too late.

Still standing beside Courtney's table, Mr. Melvin opened the bag and reached inside. His eyes narrowed in bewilderment.

Then he let out a high-pitched, startled cry as he pulled the big, black snake out.

The lunch bag dropped to the floor. The rubber snake wriggled briefly in his hand.

Molly was right. It was *very* real-looking.

Mr. Melvin let out another cry, and the snake dropped to the floor.

The room filled with startled shrieks and cries.

Courtney leapt up from her seat. She gave Mr. Melvin a gentle shove to move him out of the way. Then she began stomping on the snake. Fierce, hard stomps.

Heroic stomps.

A few seconds later, she picked the snake up

and flashed Mr. Melvin a triumphant grin. The snake was in two pieces. She had stomped off its head.

"My brother is going to *kill* me!" Molly moaned.

"Well, at least we scared Mr. Melvin," Charlene said after school. Charlene always tries to look on the bright side.

"I can't believe he spent the rest of the afternoon trying to find out who put the snake in the bag," Hat exclaimed.

"Courtney kept looking over at us," I said. "Do you think she suspected us?"

"Probably," Hat replied. "I'm just glad to get out of there."

"Mr. Melvin has a really funny scream," Charlene remarked.

Molly didn't say a word. I guessed she was thinking about what her brother would do to her when he discovered his rubber snake was gone.

We were walking to my house. We had all agreed to hold a meeting and try to come up with a better plan for scaring Courtney.

It was a beautiful, warm day. It had been raining all week. This was the rainy season in southern California. But today the sun was bright yellow in a clear, smogless sky.

Everyone was thinking about how we almost got caught — and how we failed at frightening Courtney.

We failed. And Courtney was a hero once again.

"The rubber snake was a bad idea," Hat murmured as we crossed the street onto my block.

"Tell us about it," Molly grumbled, rolling her eyes.

"Courtney will never fall for a fake," Hat continued. "We need something real to scare Courtney. Something alive."

"Huh? Something alive?" I asked.

Hat started to reply — but a woman's voice interrupted him.

I turned to see Mrs. Rudolph, one of our neighbors, running toward us. Her blonde hair was all wild, and she had a very troubled expression on her face.

"Eddie, please — you've got to help me!" she cried.

7

I felt a cold chill run down my back. Mrs. Rudolph looked so frightened.

"What's w-wrong?" I stammered.

She pointed up to the sky. "Can you help me?"

"Huh?" I followed her gaze. It took me a while to realize she was pointing up to a tree branch, not to the sky.

"It's Muttly, my cat," Mrs. Rudolph said, shielding her eyes from the sun with one hand, still pointing with the other.

"I see him," Hat said. "On that branch. The bent one."

"I don't know how he got out of the house," Mrs. Rudolph said. "He never climbs trees. Somehow he got up there, and he can't get down."

I stared up into the thick leaves. Yep. There was Muttly. Pretty high up. Making frightened yowling sounds and pawing at the slender tree branch.

We all stood staring up at the frightened cat.

28

Suddenly I felt Mrs. Rudolph's hand on my shoulder. "Can you climb up and get him, Eddie?"

I swallowed hard. I'm not the best tree climber in the world. In fact, I *hate* climbing trees. I always cut my hands on the bark or scrape the skin off my stomach or something.

"Please hurry," Mrs. Rudolph pleaded. "Muttly's so scared. He — he's going to fall."

So *what* if he falls! Aren't cats supposed to have nine lives?

That's what I thought. But I didn't say that to Mrs. Rudolph.

Instead, I stammered something about how high up he was.

"You're good at climbing trees, aren't you?" Mrs. Rudolph said. "I mean, all boys your age climb trees, don't they?" Her eyes studied me. She had a strong look of disapproval on her face.

She thinks I'm a chicken, I realized.

If I don't climb the tree and rescue her stupid cat, she'll tell my mom what a weakling I am. The word will be out all over the neighborhood: Mrs. Rudolph asked Eddie for help, and he just stood there like a coward, making lame excuses.

"I'm a little afraid of heights," I confessed.

"Go ahead, Eddie," Hat urged. "You can do it." Some friend.

Above us, the cat yowled loudly. He sounded like a baby crying. His tail stood stiffly straight up in the air.

"You can do it, Eddie," Charlene said, staring up at the cat.

"Please hurry," Mrs. Rudolph pleaded. "My kids will be heartbroken if anything happens to Muttly."

I hesitated, gazing up the long, rough-barked trunk.

The cat yowled again.

I saw the branch tremble. I saw the cat's legs scrabble frantically as he lost his grip.

Then I heard the cat *yelp* as he started to fall.

8

We all screamed.

The branch bobbed up and down. The cat clung to the branch with his front paws. Its back legs kicked the air furiously.

"Oh no oh no oh no!" Mrs. Rudolph chanted, covering her eyes with one hand.

The cat yowled in terror.

Somehow he managed to pull himself back up onto the shaking tree branch. Then he cried again, frightened, human-sounding cries.

Mrs. Rudolph lowered her hand from her eyes. She stared disgustedly at me. "I guess I'd better call the fire department."

I knew I should grab onto the tree trunk and pull myself up. But I really am afraid of heights. I'm just not a good climber.

With an exasperated sigh, Mrs. Rudolph turned and started jogging to her house. She stopped when we heard a girl's voice cry out.

"Hey — what's the problem?"

Courtney rolled onto the sidewalk on her sleek red racing bike. She hopped off and let the bike fall to the ground. She was wearing white denim overalls over a bright yellow T-shirt.

"What's going on, guys?" she asked, hurrying up to us.

"My cat — " Mrs. Rudolph said, pointing up to the tree.

The cat yowled in panic.

Courtney gazed up to the bobbing branch.

"I'll get him down," Courtney said. She grabbed the tree trunk and began shinnying up.

The cat meowed and nearly slipped again.

Courtney climbed quickly, easily, wrapping her legs around the trunk, pulling herself up with both hands.

A few seconds later, she made her way onto the branch, grabbed the cat around the stomach with one hand, and pulled him close to her body. Then she skillfully lowered herself to the ground.

"Here's the poor kitty," Courtney said, smoothing the cat's fur, petting it gently. She handed him to Mrs. Rudolph. Courtney's white denims and yellow T-shirt were smeared with dirt and bits of dark bark. She had pieces of green leaves in her blonde hair.

"Oh, thank you," Mrs. Rudolph gushed, wrapping the still mewing cat in her arms. "Thank you so much, dear. You were so wonderful."

Courtney brushed some of the dirt off her overalls. "I like climbing trees," she told Mrs. Rudolph. "It's really fun."

Mrs. Rudolph turned her gaze to me, and her smile quickly faded. "I'm glad *someone* in this neighborhood is brave," she said, making a disgusted face. She thanked Courtney again, then turned and carried the cat into the house.

I felt so bad. I wanted to sink into the ground with the worms. I wanted to disappear and never be seen again.

But there I was, standing with my hands shoved in my jeans pockets.

And there was Courtney, grinning at me. Gloating. Rubbing it in with that smug look on her face.

Hat, Molly, and Charlene didn't say a word. When I looked at them, they avoided my eyes. I knew they were embarrassed for me. And angry that Courtney had made us all look bad again.

Courtney picked up her bike and started walking it away. She threw her leg over the bar and climbed on to the seat. Then she suddenly turned back to me.

"Hey, Eddie — was it *you* who put that dumb snake in my lunch?"

"Of course not!" I exclaimed. I kicked the grass with one sneaker.

She continued to stare at me, her blue eyes studying my face.

I knew I was blushing. I could feel my cheeks grow hot. But there was nothing I could do about it.

"I thought maybe it was you," Courtney said, tossing her hair behind her shoulder. "I thought maybe you were trying to pay me back. You know. For the green snake thing."

"No way," I muttered. "No way, Courtney."

My three friends shifted uncomfortably. Hat started humming some song.

Finally, Courtney raised her feet to the pedals and rode off down the street.

"We've *got* to find a way to scare her," I said through clenched teeth as soon as she had ridden out of sight. "We've just *got* to!"

"How about a live tarantula down her back?" Hat suggested.

9

The plan was simple.

Mr. Dollinger, the science teacher, kept two tarantulas in a cage in the second-floor science lab.

Hat and I would sneak into the science lab after school on Thursday. We would borrow one of the tarantulas and hide it in my locker overnight.

The next morning, we all had gym right after morning meeting. There is a narrow balcony over the gym floor where equipment is stored. Hat and I would sneak up onto the balcony with the tarantula.

Then Molly and Charlene would start talking to Courtney and get her to stand under the balcony. When Courtney was in position under the balcony, one of us would drop the tarantula onto Courtney's head.

Then she'd scream and howl, and the tarantula would get tangled in her hair, and she wouldn't be able to get it out, so she'd scream some more and go totally ballistic, and we'd all have a good laugh.

A simple plan.

And one we were sure would work.

What could go wrong?

Thursday after school, Molly and Charlene wished us luck. Hat and I went into the shop room and pretended to be working on our wood projects. Actually, we were waiting for all the kids to leave the school building.

Pretty soon it was silent out in the hall. I poked my head out the shop door. Empty.

"Okay, Hat," I whispered, motioning for him to follow me. "Let's get this over with."

We crept out into the hall. Our shoes scraped noisily against the hard tile floor. The halls at school are kind of creepy when everyone has left and it's so quiet.

We passed by the teachers' lounge near the front stairway. The door was open a crack, and I could hear some kind of teachers' meeting going on.

That's great, I told myself. If the teachers are all meeting downstairs, we will have the science lab to ourselves.

Hat and I hurried up the front stairs. We leaned on the banister and tried to move as silently as we could.

The science lab is at the end of the hall on the

second floor. We passed by a couple of eighth graders we didn't know. But we didn't see anyone else. There didn't seem to be any teachers up there. They were probably all at the meeting.

Hat and I peeked into the lab. Late afternoon sunlight poured in through the windows. We had to squint down the long rows of lab tables.

"Mr. Dollinger?" I called. I just wanted to make sure he wasn't there.

No reply.

We both tried to squeeze through the door at the same time, but we didn't fit. Hat laughed. His nervous, high-pitched giggle. I raised a finger to my lips, signaling for him to be quiet. I didn't want anyone to hear us.

Hat followed me down the center aisle of the long room. My heart began to thud loudly in my chest. My eyes darted around the room.

The sunlight seemed to grow even brighter. The watercolor paintings of the rain forest we had all made were hanging on the wall behind Mr. Dollinger's desk. Water dripped in one of the lab sinks to our right. *Plonk. Plonk. Plonk.*

The door to the tall metal supply cabinet beside Mr. Dollinger's desk had been left open. I pointed it out to Hat. "That probably means he's coming back up here after the teachers' meeting," I whispered.

Mr. Dollinger is a neat freak. He wouldn't leave a supply closet open overnight.

Hat gave me a shove. "We'd better hurry."

"Don't push me," I grumbled.

We made our way to the tarantula cage, on a metal table against the wall. It was actually a rectangular, plywood box with a wire mesh top.

A loud crash made me stop a few feet from the cage. I gasped and turned to Hat. "What was that?"

The sound repeated. We both realized it was a venetian blind, blown by the wind, banging against the open window behind us.

I breathed a long sigh of relief. I stared at Hat and he stared at me. He nervously adjusted his baseball cap over his forehead. "Eddie, maybe this isn't such a good idea," he whispered. "Maybe we should get out of here."

I was tempted to agree with Hat and run out the door as fast as I could. But then I remembered Courtney's smug smile as she climbed down from the tree with the cat. "Let's stick to the plan," I said.

I really wanted to scare Courtney. More than anything else in the world.

Hat and I peered down through the wire mesh at the two tarantulas. The bigger one was crawling along one end of the cage. The smaller, browner one was sitting like a lump at the other end.

"Yuck," I said in a low voice. "They really are gross."

Their legs were all hairy and prickly-looking. Their bodies looked like disgusting brown hairy sacks.

"Let's take the big one," Hat urged, reaching for the lid. A grin spread across his face. "It'll make a nice *plop* when it lands on Courtney's head."

We both laughed. Hat made some funny plopping sounds.

He lifted up the wire mesh top of the cage. He reached a hand in to grab the bigger tarantula. Then he suddenly stopped, and his grin faded.

"We've got a little problem," he said.

"Huh? What?" I glanced nervously back to the doorway. No one there.

"What are we going to put it in?" Hat demanded.

My mouth dropped open. "Oh."

"We forgot to bring something to put it in," Hat said. He lowered the top of the cage. Both tarantulas were crawling slowly toward each other now.

"Yeah. Well, we need a bag or something," I said. My eyes searched the tabletops.

"A bag isn't any good," Hat replied, frowning. "Tarantulas can tear right through a bag."

"Oh, yeah. You're right."

"Why didn't we think of this before?" Hat demanded. "Why were we so stupid? What did we think we were doing? You can't just put a tarantula in your backpack and carry it around!"

"Calm down," I said, motioning for him to lower his voice. I could see he was starting to panic. "There must be *something* to keep a tarantula in up here."

"This is really stupid," he grumbled. "Did you think I was going to keep it in my pocket?"

"Wait," I told him. I hurried over to the next table and picked up a plastic container. It was the size of a cottage cheese container and had a plastic top. "This is perfect," I whispered, holding it up to show him. "I'll just poke holes in the top."

"Hurry," Hat urged. He pulled off his cap and scratched his dark hair.

I poked several air holes in the lid with a pencil. Then I carried the plastic container over to the cage. "Here," I said, handing it to him.

"You have to hold it," Hat told me. "I can't hold the container and pick up the tarantula."

"Oh," I replied unhappily. I didn't want to be that close to the tarantula.

My hand started shaking a little. But I held the container close to the cage, ready to snap the lid over it as soon as Hat dropped one of the ugly creatures inside.

He pulled up the lid and reached into the cage. Hat was really brave. He wrapped his hand around the bigger one's body and lifted it up easily. Hat didn't even hesitate or make a disgusted face.

I was impressed.

I nearly dropped the plastic container when he lowered the tarantula inside. My hand was really shaking. But I managed to hold on.

The tarantula began flopping around frantically, shooting its legs out, slipping and sliding on the slippery plastic surface.

"He doesn't like it in there," I said in a trembling voice.

"Too bad," Hat replied, closing the wire mesh cage lid. "Quick, Eddie — put the lid on the container."

I scrambled to clamp the lid on.

I almost had it in place when I heard footsteps outside the door. And voices.

Hat and I both gasped as we realized Mr. Dollinger was about to walk in.

A feeble croak escaped my lips. The bright sunlight suddenly glared white. I felt the floor sway.

I could feel my panic weigh me down. I suddenly felt as if I weighed a thousand pounds.

I could hear Mr. Dollinger talking to another teacher right outside the science lab door. In another few seconds, he'd step inside, and . . . and . . .

"Quick — duck under the table!" Hat whispered, his eyes wide with fright beneath his cap.

I started to follow him under the table. But I realized it wasn't a good hiding place at all. Mr. Dollinger would see us as soon as he went to his desk.

"No — no good!" I croaked. "No good. Uh . . ."

My eyes flashed around the room. Where could we hide? Where?

"The supply cabinet!" I cried. I grabbed Hat's arm and pulled him with me.

The tall metal cabinet was wide enough to hide both of us.

Could we get into it in time?

We scrambled inside, pushing each other forward.

I pulled the door closed. It clicked shut just as Mr. Dollinger entered the room.

Hat and I stood trembling in the darkness of the cabinet, listening to his footsteps approach. I gripped the tarantula container tightly in one hand.

Mr. Dollinger was softly humming a tune. I heard him stop right in front of the supply cabinet.

My heart was pounding so loud, I wondered if the teacher could hear it through the cabinet door.

I shifted my weight and bumped into Hat. There wasn't another inch of space in there. I could hear Hat's shallow breathing. I could tell he was as scared as I was.

What if Mr. Dollinger decided to open the cabinet door?

Please, please — just turn out the lights and go home, I pleaded silently.

I could hear him shuffling papers on his desk. I heard the desk drawer open and shut. I heard a book slam shut. More footsteps. Water running in one of the sinks.

He turned off the water. He was still humming softly to himself. More footsteps. The click of the light switch.

Then silence.

I struggled to hear over my pounding heart-beat. Silence. No humming. No footsteps.

Hat and I stood frozen in the darkness, listening hard. "He — he's gone," I stammered finally. "He left, Hat."

"Phewwww!" Hat sighed loudly.

"Let's get out of here!" I cried. I reached for the latch.

My hand fumbled around in the darkness, sweeping over the metal door. I located a slender metal bar and pulled up on it. It didn't budge.

"Hey — " I cried out. I moved my hand slowly up the door, trying to find a latch or release.

"Hurry up. Open the cabinet door," Hat urged. "It's getting hot in here."

"I know," I replied tensely. "I — I can't find anything."

"Let me try," Hat said impatiently. He pushed my hand away and began fumbling with the metal bar.

"There's got to be a latch or something," I said shrilly.

"Very helpful," Hat grumbled. He began pounding on the door with his open hand.

I grabbed his arm. "Stop. That won't open it. And someone will hear you."

"*You* try again," he ordered. His voice sounded really tiny and afraid.

I swallowed hard. I suddenly had a heavy lump

in my throat. It felt as if my heart had leapt up into my neck.

I fumbled frantically with everything I could grab hold of. But I couldn't find anything that would open the door.

"I give up. We — we're locked in, Hat," I stammered.

"I don't believe it," he muttered.

The container started to slip out of my hand. I grabbed it with both hands — and made a startling discovery.

The lid had come off.

"Oh, no," I murmured.

"What now?" Hat demanded.

Taking a deep breath, I shook the container.

It was empty. No tarantula.

I tried to tell Hat that the tarantula had escaped, but my voice caught in my throat. I let out a choking sound.

And then I felt a prickling on my leg just above my sock.

And then another prickling, like a pinprick, a little higher up.

"Hat — the tarantula — " I managed to croak. "It — it's crawling up my leg."

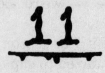

11

The pinpricks moved a little higher on my leg.

I could feel the tarantula's warm, hairy body rub against my skin.

"It — it's going to b-bite me," I stuttered. "I *know* it is."

"Don't move," Hat advised, sounding even more frightened than me. "Just don't move."

The creature's legs dug into my skin, like sharp needles.

"I — I have to get *out* of here!" I screamed. Without thinking about it, I lowered my shoulder and heaved all my weight against the cabinet door.

With a loud *pop*, it swung open.

A startled cry escaped my lips as I tumbled out. I landed hard on my side, and the empty plastic container rolled across the room.

Breathing hard, I scrambled to my feet and began furiously kicking and shaking my leg.

The tarantula dropped to the floor and immediately began scrabbling across the linoleum. "Catch it! Catch it!" I shrieked.

Hat dove out of the cabinet and lurched after the tarantula.

I grabbed up the container and hurried over to him. Hat lifted the tarantula high in the air. Its hairy legs kicked and squirmed, but Hat didn't let go.

He plopped the ugly thing into the container. "Put the lid on tight this time," he warned.

"Don't worry," I moaned. My hands were shaking. But I clamped the lid on tightly, then checked and rechecked it three times.

A short while later, Hat and I were heading downstairs to deposit the tarantula in my locker for safekeeping. I could still feel the itchy pinpricks on my leg, even though I knew the tarantula hadn't bitten me.

"Wow. That was scary!" Hat declared. "That was really scary."

"It just means that the rest of the plan will go perfectly," I assured him.

A little before nine the next morning, Hat and I were hiding again. This time we were hiding on the narrow balcony that overlooks the gym.

While everyone else in our class changed into their gym shorts and sweats and stuff, Hat and I sneaked out of the boys' locker room. Hat hid the

47

tarantula container under his sweatshirt, and we hurried up to the balcony.

The four of us had been calling each other for most of the night, getting the plan straight. It was a very simple plan, actually.

All Molly and Charlene had to do was get Courtney to stand under the balcony. Then Hat would drop the tarantula into her hair, and we'd all watch her scream and cry and carry on, and make a total fool of herself.

Simple.

"What if Courtney doesn't get upset?" Molly had asked me on the phone. "What if she just plucks it out of her hair and calmly asks if anyone has lost a tarantula?"

"That's impossible," I had replied. "Courtney is calm — but she isn't *that* calm! She's *got* to scream and go wild with a tarantula in her hair. If she doesn't, she's not human. She's a statue or something."

"Ready, Hat?" I asked, peering over the side of the balcony.

He nodded solemnly, his eyes on the volleyball nets below.

He carefully pulled the lid off the container. The tarantula reached up two legs as if to grab him.

I heard voices down below. A few girls had wandered out of their locker room onto the floor. One of them picked up a volleyball and took a jump shot at the basket. The ball hit the rim and bounced off.

"Get down. They can see you," Hat whispered.

I lowered my head. It was hot up on the balcony, hotter than down on the gym floor, and I started to sweat.

We were both on our knees. Hat was holding the tarantula container in front of him with both hands.

I could hear more voices down below. Several boys had come out and were dribbling a volleyball up and down the floor, passing it off to one another.

"Do you see Courtney?" Hat whispered.

I raised myself a little higher and peered down. "Yes!"

Molly and Charlene had Courtney between them. Both of them were talking excitedly at the same time. I couldn't hear what they were talking about.

Courtney was shaking her head. I saw her laugh, then shake her head some more. She was wearing a loose-fitting purple T-shirt, and white shorts over purple tights. Her blonde hair was tied behind her in a loose ponytail.

A perfect target, I thought gleefully. I grinned at Hat. I had a good feeling about this. A very good feeling.

Raising my eyes beyond the volleyball nets, I

saw that Mr. Russo, the gym teacher, was talking to another teacher at the door.

Good, I thought. We don't want Mr. Russo blowing the whistle and starting the volleyball game until we take care of Courtney.

Molly and Charlene, meanwhile, still had Courtney between them. They were still chatting away. As they talked, they kept backing up, backing up, until they were almost in position.

"Just a few more feet and Courtney will be under the balcony," I whispered to Hat. "It's happening, Hat. It's really happening."

I was so excited, I felt like I was about to burst. Beads of sweat rolled down my forehead and into my eyes. I wiped it with the sleeve of my T-shirt and peered down.

Yes!

Molly and Charlene had done it. They had backed Courtney under the balcony. The three of them stood right beneath us.

Perfect!

"Hat — do it!" I whispered.

Hat didn't hesitate. Not for a second. This was too perfect. Too perfect!

His eyes on the three girls directly below, he reached into the container and picked up the hairy tarantula.

Then he raised himself up a little higher over the balcony edge, held the tarantula over the side, took careful aim — and let it drop.

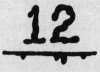

12

Hat and I both leaned over the balcony and watched the tarantula drop.

And we both cried out in horror when it landed with a sick *plop* in Molly's hair.

"Hat — you missed!" I screamed.

But Molly was screaming a lot louder. Her face was as red as a tomato, and her eyes were bulging out of her head. She was shrieking at the top of her lungs and doing a strange dance, hopping wildly up and down while her hands thrashed the air.

A lot of kids were running over with startled and bewildered expressions. "What's wrong with Molly?" someone screamed.

"Why is she doing that?"

"What happened to her?"

Staring down, I leaned so far over the balcony, I nearly dropped like the tarantula.

Poor Molly was tearing at her hair now, still shrieking and hopping around.

I cried out in relief as she finally managed to pull the tarantula from her dark hair. She juggled it in her hand, nearly dropping it. Then, still screaming, she tossed it to Charlene!

Beside me on the balcony, Hat was laughing now. But I was too upset to find it funny.

How could Hat have missed such an easy shot?

Charlene let out a scream that rattled the gym rafters. She bobbled the tarantula from one hand to the other.

Then it dropped to the floor at her feet.

Charlene leapt back, still screaming, both hands pressed against the sides of her face.

Everyone in the gym class had huddled around. Some kids still looked confused. Others were laughing. A couple of girls were trying to comfort Molly, whose hair was standing straight up on her head.

"Oh, wow. Oh, wow," Hat kept repeating, shaking his head. "Oh, wow."

Gripping the balcony edge with both hands, I watched Courtney bend over and gently pick up the tarantula from the gym floor. She placed it in the palm of her hand and appeared to be saying soothing words to it.

The kids had formed a circle around Courtney. As she held the tarantula close to her face, they quieted down and watched.

"It's just a tarantula," Courtney said, petting its hairy back with one finger. "Tarantulas don't bite that often. And if they do, it doesn't hurt very much."

Kids began murmuring once again about how brave Courtney was. I saw Molly and Charlene comforting each other at the edge of the circle. Charlene was smoothing down Molly's hair. Molly's whole body was still quivering.

"Where did this tarantula come from?" Courtney was asking.

I saw Molly stare up angrily at us. She raised her fist and shook it toward us.

I ducked down out of sight behind the balcony wall.

"The plan didn't work too well," Hat murmured.

Is he the master of understatement — or what?

We didn't realize that the disaster wasn't over. "Let's get out of here," I whispered.

Too late. We both looked up to see Mr. Russo glaring angrily at us from the balcony entrance. "What are you boys doing up here?" he asked suspiciously.

I turned to Hat. Hat stared back at me blankly.

Neither of us could think of a good answer.

"Come on back downstairs," Mr. Russo said softly, holding open the door for us. "Let's have a nice, long talk."

It could have been worse, I thought.

Sure, Hat and I had to stay after school and clean the science lab every afternoon for the next two weeks. And sure, we had to write one-thousand-word essays on why it's wrong to steal living things and drop them on people's heads.

And sure, Molly and Charlene aren't speaking to Hat *or* me.

But it could have been worse.

I mean, what if Hat and I were still locked in the supply cabinet? *That* would be worse, wouldn't it?

It was later that afternoon. I was slumped on my bed, glumly thinking about gym class and how our plan had bombed.

It's all Courtney's fault, I told myself, absently pulling at a little tear in my bedspread.

Courtney had moved just at the last minute.

She *must* have moved. Hat couldn't be *that* bad of an aim.

I sighed bitterly as once again I pictured Courtney calmly picking the tarantula up off the floor and petting it. *"It's only a tarantula,"* Courtney had said. So smug. So superior. *"It's only a tarantula. They don't bite very often."*

Why didn't it bite her hand?

That would have wiped the smug expression off her face.

Why did she have to be so totally brave?

Courtney really deserves to be scared out of her wits, I thought unhappily. I tore at the little rip in the bedspread, turning it into a big rip.

She's really *asking* for it, asking to be frightened speechless.

But how, how, how?

Sitting on the edge of the bed, I had my head lowered and my shoulders hunched. I was leaning forward glumly, picking at the bedspread without even realizing it.

Again I pictured Hat letting the tarantula drop.

Again I saw it land on Molly's head.

No! No! No!

Again I saw Molly start to do her frantic, furious dance.

The unhappy picture vanished from my mind as I suddenly realized I was no longer alone. Raising my eyes to the doorway, I gasped sharply.

And saw the tall, lean monster stagger toward me, its face dripping with dark blood.

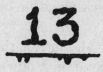

13

The tall monster lurched toward me, its dripping arms reaching out in front of it, ready to grab me.

"Kevin — get *out* of here!" I cried. "You're dripping mud all over my floor!"

My older brother Kevin lowered his arms to his sides. "It isn't real mud, punk," he said. "It's makeup."

"I don't care," I replied shrilly, jumping up off the bed and giving him a hard shove in the stomach. "It's dripping all over."

He laughed. "Scared you, didn't I?"

"No way!" I insisted. "I knew it was you."

"You thought it was a Mud Monster," he said, grinning at me through the thick, brownish-orange gunk dripping down his face. "Admit it, punk."

I hate when he calls me punk. I guess that's why he does it. "You don't look like a Mud Monster," I told him nastily. "You just look like a pile of garbage."

"We scared some little kids who came into the woods this afternoon," Kevin said gleefully. "You should've seen their faces. We ran at them and yelled BOO. Two of them started to cry." He snickered.

"Way to go," I muttered. I gave him another shove toward the door and got the thick, brownish-orange gunk all over my hands.

"The video is almost finished," he told me, deliberately wiping his hand on my open notebook. He stared down at the dark stain he had made on my math homework. "Maybe I'll let you see it when it's done."

"Get away from my stuff, Kevin!" I said angrily. Then I remembered what I wanted to ask him, and changed my tone. "Can I be in the video?" I pleaded. "Please? You said maybe I could be in it — remember?"

"Huh-uh, punk." He shook his head. "You'd get too scared."

"What?" Was he putting me on?

"You'd get too scared, Eddie," he repeated, scratching his forehead through the heavy, wet makeup. "All alone in the deep, dark woods with three Mud Monsters walking around. You'd lose it. You'd totally lose it."

"Hey — " I cried angrily. "You're not funny, Kevin. You promised — "

"No, I didn't," Kevin insisted. A big brown blob of gunk fell off his shoulder and landed with a *splat* on my floor. "Whoa. You're going to have to clean that up," he said, grinning meanly.

"I'm going to make you *eat* it!" I shouted angrily, crossing my arms over my chest.

He just laughed.

I suddenly had an idea. "Kevin, will you help me with something?" I asked thoughtfully.

"Probably not," he replied, still grinning. "What is it?"

"Do you have any good ideas for scaring someone?" I asked.

He narrowed his eyes at me. Then he gestured to the brownish-orange stuff covering his whole body. "Isn't this scary enough?"

"No. I mean, some other way to scare someone," I said, wondering how to explain. I decided just to come right out and say it. "Some friends and I, we're trying to scare this girl, Courtney."

"Why?" Kevin demanded, resting a globby hand on my dresser top.

"You know. Just for fun," I told him.

He nodded.

"But we haven't been able to scare her at all," I continued. "Everything we try totally bombs out." I sank back onto my bed.

"What have you tried?" Kevin asked.

"Oh. A couple of things. A snake and a tarantula," I said. "But she didn't get scared."

"Too small," he muttered. He stepped away

from the dresser. I could see that he had left a big brown stain on the side.

"Huh? What do you mean 'too small'?" I demanded.

"Too small," he repeated. "You're trying to scare her with little things. You've got to scare her with something big. You know. Maybe something bigger than she is."

I thought about what he was saying. It seemed to make sense. "What do you mean by big?" I asked him. "You mean like an elephant?"

He frowned and shook his head. "Eddie, where are you going to get an elephant? I mean like a big dog. You know. A huge, growling dog."

"A dog?" I scratched my head.

"Yeah. Let's say this girl Courtney is walking down the street, or she's in the woods, maybe — and suddenly she hears angry growls and snarls. She looks up and sees this enormous dog, its mouth open, its fangs bared, running right at her. That'll scare her. No problem."

"Not bad," I said thoughtfully. "Not bad. You're a genius, Kevin. Really."

"Tell me about it," he replied. He walked out of the room, leaving a muddy trail behind him.

A huge, growling dog, I thought. I pictured it in my mind. I pictured it raising its head to the moon and howling like a wolf.

Then I pictured Courtney walking innocently

down a dark street. She hears a sound. A low growl. She stops. Her eyes grow wide with fear.

What's that noise? she wonders.

And then she sees it. The biggest, meanest, loudest, angriest dog that ever lived. Its eyes glow red. It pulls back its heavy lips to reveal a mouth full of pointy fangs.

With an earth-shattering growl, it makes its leap. It goes right for her throat.

Courtney cries out for help. Then she turns. She's running now, running for her life, shrieking and crying like a frightened baby.

"Here, boy," I call to the attacking beast.

The dog stops. It turns around. It walks quickly to me, its tail wagging. Courtney is still crying, still shaking all over, as the dog gently licks my hand.

"It's only a dog," I tell her. "Dogs won't hurt you — unless they sense that you're *afraid!*"

I jumped up from my bed, laughing out loud.

It's definitely worth a try, I thought excitedly. Definitely worth a try.

Now, who do I know who has an enormous, growling, ferocious dog?

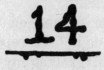

14

Saturday afternoon we were in Charlene's back yard, trying out the new croquet set her father had bought. It was an overcast day. High clouds kept blocking out the sun, sending long, gray shadows over the back lawn.

The roar of a power mower from next door made it a little hard to be heard. But I was telling Molly, Charlene, and Hat about my brother's idea for scaring Courtney.

"A big, angry dog is way scary," Hat quickly agreed. He tapped his mallet hard against his green croquet ball and sent mine sailing into the hedge.

Molly frowned. She still hadn't forgiven me for the tarantula incident, even though I had apologized a thousand times. She straightened the bottom of her yellow T-shirt over her black Lycra bike shorts and prepared to take her turn.

"We need a dog that really looks vicious," Molly said. She slammed her ball hard. It missed the hoop and bounced off a wooden peg.

"I guess my dog, Buttercup, could do it," Charlene offered, sighing.

"Huh? Buttercup?" I cried out in surprise. "Get serious, Charlene. Buttercup is a big, lovable oaf. He couldn't scare a fly."

A teasing smile formed on Charlene's face. "Buttercup could do it," she repeated.

"Oh, sure," I said, rolling my eyes. "He's real vicious. That's why you gave him a vicious name like Buttercup."

"It's your turn," Molly said to me, pointing to my ball way over at the hedge.

"This is such a boring game," I complained. "Why does anyone like it?"

"I like it," Hat said. He was winning.

Charlene cupped her hands around her mouth and shouted, "Buttercup! Buttercup! Come here, you ferocious beast!"

A few seconds later, the big Saint Bernard came lumbering toward us from the side of the house. His bushy, white tail was wagging hard, making his entire backside waggle as he hurried across the grass, his big pink tongue drooping out.

"Ooh, I'm scared! I'm scared!" I cried sarcastically. I dropped my croquet mallet and hugged myself, pretending to shiver in fright.

Buttercup ignored me. He ran up to Charlene and started licking her hand, making tiny mewing sounds, almost like a cat.

"Ooh, he's tough," I exclaimed.

Hat came up beside me, adjusting his baseball cap over his eyes. "He's a big, lovable Saint Bernard, Charlene," Hat said, bending to scratch the dog behind the ears. "He's not too scary. We need a big wolf. Or a six-foot-tall Doberman."

Buttercup turned his big head to lick Hat's hand.

"Yuck!" Hat made a disgusted face. "I hate dog slobber."

"Where can we get a real attack dog?" I asked, picking up my mallet and leaning on it like a cane. "Do we know anyone who has a guard dog? A big, ugly German shepherd, maybe?"

Charlene still had that teasing grin on her face, as if she knew something the rest of us didn't. "Give Buttercup a chance," she said softly. "You might be surprised."

Clouds drifted over the sun again. The air suddenly grew cooler as gray shadows slid over the grass.

The power mower on the other side of the hedge sputtered to a stop. The back yard suddenly seemed eerily quiet and still.

Buttercup dropped to the grass and rolled onto his back. His four furry paws kicked the air as he scratched his back on the lawn.

"Not too impressive, Charlene," Hat said, laughing. The dog looked so stupid.

"I haven't done our little trick yet," Charlene replied. "Just watch."

She turned to the dog and started to whistle. A tuneless whistle, just a bunch of shrill, flat tones.

The big Saint Bernard reacted immediately. As soon as he heard Charlene's whistle, he rolled off his back and climbed to his feet. His tail shot out stiffly behind him. His entire body appeared to go rigid. His ears stood up on his head.

Charlene continued to whistle. Not loudly. A steady, low whistle of long, shrill notes.

And as we stared in silent surprise, Buttercup began to growl. The growl started deep in his stomach, angry and menacing.

He pulled back his dark lips. He bared his big teeth.

He growled loudly. His growl became a vicious snarl.

The dog's eyes glowed angrily. His back stiffened. His head arched back as if preparing to attack.

Charlene sucked in a deep breath and whistled some more. Her eyes were locked on the growling dog.

"Buttercup — get Eddie!" Charlene suddenly screamed. "Get Eddie! Kill! *Kill!*"

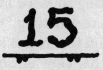

15

"No!" I shrieked and fell back toward the hedge.

The dog growled a warning. Then it leapt to attack.

I raised my arms in front of me as a shield and waited for the impact.

And waited.

When I slowly lowered my arms, I saw that Charlene was hugging the dog around the neck. Charlene had a gleeful grin on her face. Buttercup turned and planted a slobbery dog kiss on her forehead.

"Gotcha, Eddie!" Charlene declared. "That was to pay you back for the tarantula."

Molly laughed. "Way to go, Charlene."

"Wow," I exclaimed weakly. My heart was still pounding. The back yard was spinning in front of me.

"That's a good trick," Hat told Charlene. "How did you teach him that?"

"I didn't," Charlene said, giving the dog a final

hug, then shoving him away from her. "It was sort of an accident. I was whistling one day, and Buttercup went ballistic on me. He started growling and snarling, showing his teeth."

"I guess he really hates the way you whistle!" I exclaimed, starting to feel a little more normal.

"He hates *anyone* whistling," Charlene replied, brushing dog fur off the legs of her denim cutoffs. "Maybe it hurts his ears or something. I don't know. But you can see what it makes him do. He goes nuts like that every time someone whistles."

"That's great!" Hat declared.

"He really *can* terrify Courtney," Molly said.

We watched the dog lumber away, his tongue hanging nearly to the ground. He sniffed at something in the flower bed, then disappeared around the side of the house.

"Poor dog," Charlene said, shaking her head. "He hates California. He's hot all the time. But when we moved here from Michigan, we just couldn't bear to part with him."

"I'm glad you didn't," I said enthusiastically. "Now we're finally going to scare the *life* out of Courtney!"

Molly tapped a croquet ball softly with her mallet. She had a troubled expression on her face. "We're not really going to *hurt* Courtney, are we?" she asked. "I mean, Buttercup isn't really going to attack her, is he? If he gets out of control . . ."

"Of course not," Charlene answered quickly. "He stops growling and carrying on as soon as I stop whistling. Really. As soon as the whistling stops, he goes right back to his gentle personality."

Molly looked relieved. She tapped the ball through a hoop, then used the mallet to push it back out.

We had all lost interest in the croquet game. Planning how we were going to use Buttercup to terrify Courtney was a lot more exciting than any game.

The sun had poked out from the high clouds. The closely trimmed grass gleamed brightly in the sunlight. We tossed down the mallets and made our way to the shade of the big grapefruit tree in the center of the back yard.

"We should scare Courtney in the woods, at that tree house she and Denise built by Muddy Creek," I suggested, sprawling on my back on the grass. "It's the perfect place. She and Denise all alone in the woods. Suddenly, a snarling dog leaps out at them. They'll both scream for a week!"

"Yeah, that's good," Hat agreed. "In the woods, there are plenty of places for us to hide and watch. I mean, Charlene can hide behind a bush or an evergreen or something and whistle her brains out. We'll all be hidden. Courtney will never know who did it."

Sitting with her legs crossed, Molly chewed her

lower lip thoughtfully. She pushed her glasses up on her nose. "I don't like it," she said. "It's no fun if we don't scare Courtney in front of a lot of people. If we scare her in the woods with no one around, who will care?"

"*We* will!" I argued. "*We* will see it. That's all that counts. *We* will know that we finally managed to terrify her."

"And maybe we can all jump out and yell 'Gotcha!' and stuff, so she'll know we saw her get frightened," Charlene added enthusiastically. "Then we'll spread it around school, and everyone will know."

"I like it!" Hat declared.

"When should we do it?" Molly asked.

"How about *now*?" I said, jumping to my feet.

"Huh? Now?" Charlene reacted with surprise.

"Why not?" I argued. "Let's just go do it. Maybe we'll get lucky and find Courtney and Denise at their tree house. They go there a lot on weekends, you know, to hang out and read and stuff."

"Yeah! Let's go!" Hat jumped up and slapped me on the back. "Let's do it!"

"I'll go get Buttercup's leash," Charlene said. "I guess there's no reason to wait." She turned to Molly, who was hanging back.

"I have a better idea," Molly said, pulling a blade of grass from her brown hair. "Before we go running off to the woods, let's make sure that Courtney is at the tree house."

"Huh? How do we do that?" I asked.

"Simple," she replied. And then Molly did the most amazing impersonation of Denise. *"Hello, Courtney. Meet me at the tree house in ten minutes, okay?"* It was incredible! She sounded just like Denise!

We all gaped at her in amazement.

"Molly, I didn't know you were so talented," Charlene said, laughing.

"I've been practicing," Molly said. "I can do all kinds of voices. I'm really pretty good at it."

"Molly, maybe you can do cartoon voices when you get older," I suggested. "You could be Daffy Duck. You sound a lot like him already!"

Hat laughed. Molly stuck her tongue out at me.

"Let's go inside and call Courtney," Charlene said eagerly, sliding open the screen door. "If she isn't home, she's probably already at the tree house. So we'll get Buttercup and go there. If she *is* home, Molly can pretend to be Denise and tell Courtney to meet at the tree house."

We made our way into the kitchen. Charlene handed the kitchen phone to Molly. Then she brought over the cordless phone for the rest of us to listen in on.

Molly punched in Courtney's number, and we each held our breath as we listened to the phone ring. One ring. Two.

Courtney picked it up after the second ring. "Hello?"

Molly put on her best Denise voice. "Hi, Courtney. It's me." She really sounded just like Denise. I think she could've fooled Denise's own mother!

"Can you meet me in the woods? You know. At the tree house?" Molly asked in Denise's voice.

"Who *is* this?" Courtney demanded.

"It's me, of course. Denise," Molly replied.

"That's weird," we all heard Courtney say. "How can *you* be Denise when Denise is standing here right next to me?"

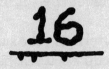

16

"Oops. Wrong number," Molly said. She quickly slammed down the receiver.

Calling Courtney had turned out to be a bad idea.

Our plan hadn't exactly worked. But we were sure we could scare Courtney with Buttercup. We just had to catch her in the woods at the right time.

The next day, Sunday, it rained. I was very disappointed.

My brother, Kevin, stood beside me at the window, watching the raindrops patter against the glass. He was very disappointed, too. He and his friends had planned to finish their Mud Monsters video in the woods.

"Today we were going to tape the big finish where the Mud Monsters rise up out of the mud," he said.

"Maybe the rain will stop," I told him.

"It doesn't matter," Kevin sighed. "We won't be able to shoot anyway."

"Why not?" I asked.

"Too muddy," he replied.

The week dragged by. It rained just about every day.

On Saturday afternoon, the sun came out. Charlene put Buttercup on a leash, and we eagerly headed to the woods.

"Courtney's *got* to be there. She's *got* to!" I declared.

"Someone has to scout out the tree house," Molly said. "Someone has to make sure Courtney and Denise are there before we let Buttercup go."

"I'll do it!" Hat and I volunteered in unison.

Everyone laughed. We were in a good mood. I think we all had a really good feeling, a feeling that this was the day we were finally going to scare Courtney out of her wits.

The woods started a few blocks from Charlene's house. It was a really pretty day, the first all week. Everything smelled fresh and sweet from all the rain.

Buttercup kept stopping to sniff flowers and bushes and other plants. Charlene had to keep tugging the leash to keep him walking. It was a tough job. It isn't easy to tug a Saint Bernard if he doesn't want to be tugged!

"My mouth is kind of dry," Charlene complained

as we neared the edge of the woods. "I hope I can whistle okay."

She tried whistling. It came out real breathy. Not much whistle sound.

But that didn't seem to matter to Buttercup. He raised his head instantly. His ears shot up and his tail stood straight back.

Charlene blew harder, but she still wasn't getting much sound.

Buttercup's stomach began to rumble. The rumble became a low growl. The growl became a snarl as the big dog ferociously bared his teeth.

"Charlene — stop," I said. "Don't waste it."

Charlene stopped whistling. The dog relaxed.

"Does anyone have some gum?" Charlene asked, holding her throat. "My mouth is really dry."

Molly handed her a stick of gum.

"Buttercup is ready!" Hat declared happily as we stepped into the woods.

Shadows of the leaves overhead danced on the ground. Sparkling rays of sunlight beamed down through the trees. Twigs and dried leaves crackled under our sneakers as we walked.

"Come on, dog!" Charlene pleaded, tugging hard at the leash.

"Ssshh," Molly warned. "We've got to be quiet now. If Courtney is in the woods, she'll hear us."

"Come on, Buttercup!" Charlene repeated in a loud whisper.

The dog was being difficult. He kept stopping to sniff things. He pulled at the leash, trying to break free and go off on his own. I guess there were too many exciting smells for him. His tail was wagging back and forth, and he was panting noisily.

We were deep in the woods now, approaching the creek. It grew shadier and cooler. Purple shadows surrounded us as we walked.

"I'll sneak up near the tree house and see if Courtney and Denise are there," I whispered. I handed the brown paper bag I'd been carrying to Hat. "Hold this for me. I'll be right back."

Hat gazed suspiciously at the bag. "What's in it?"

"You'll see," I told him and hurried off on my scouting mission. Keeping low, I made my way through a clump of tall weeds.

I glanced back at my friends. They had clustered around Buttercup. The big dog had plopped down on the ground and was chewing on a big stick.

As I followed a narrow dirt path through the trees, I realized my heart was pounding excitedly. This was it! The day of our victory over Courtney.

Her tree house was perched near the creek on the other side of a small, grassy clearing. As I approached the clearing, I could hear the soft trickle of water from the creekbed.

Slipping between the trees, I kept in the shadows. I didn't want to be spotted by Courtney or Denise. That would spoil the surprise.

A smile broke over my face as I thought about how scared they were about to become. *If* they were there. . . .

I stopped at the edge of the clearing and peered across it. The tall grass was matted down by dozens of footprints. I realized that my brother and his friends must have taped part of their Mud Monsters video there.

Keeping under the trees, I began to make my way around the circle of the clearing. There, on the other side, Courtney's tree house came into view. It looked like a large wooden crate, perched in the lowest limb of an old oak tree. A rope ladder connected it to the ground.

Were they there? Courtney and Denise?

I couldn't see them.

I took a few more steps, pushing tall weeds out of the way as I came nearer. "Ow," I muttered as something prickled my shoulder. Glancing down, I carefully pulled two burrs from the sleeve of my T-shirt.

Then I kept walking, trying to be silent as I moved nearer the tree house.

I stopped when I heard voices. Girls' voices.

And then I saw Courtney and Denise. They were just ahead of me, walking in the woods.

I ducked low behind a clump of thick shrubs.

They were only a few feet in front of me. Had they seen me?

No.

They were talking excitedly, having some kind of heated discussion. I watched them through the shrub. They were both wearing blue midriff tops and white denim shorts. Twins.

They were walking slowly in the other direction, casually pulling up weeds and wildflowers as they walked.

Great! I thought. This is *perfect!*

I *knew* this was the day!

I turned and silently hurried away. I couldn't wait to get back to my friends.

I found them in the same spot, still huddled around the dog. "Buttercup, do your stuff!" I cried excitedly, grinning and waving as I ran up to them.

"You mean they're there?" Hat asked, surprised.

"They're there," I said breathlessly, "waiting to be scared."

"Great!" Molly and Charlene exclaimed. Charlene tried to tug Buttercup to his feet.

"Wait," I said. I grabbed the brown paper bag from Hat. "Before Buttercup gets up, let's put this on first."

I pulled out the can of shaving cream I had brought.

"What's that for?" Hat demanded.

"I thought we'd smear shaving cream around his mouth," I explained. "You know. Make him look like he's frothing. Rabid dogs always froth at the mouth. When they see a growling dog frothing up white stuff as he attacks them, Courtney and Denise will drop dead!"

"Excellent!" Molly cried, slapping me on the back. "That's really excellent!"

Everyone congratulated me. Sometimes I do have great ideas, I have to admit.

Buttercup lumbered to his feet. He started pulling Charlene toward the clearing.

"Let him get closer to them," Charlene whispered loudly, as the big dog trotted through the trees, dragging her with him. "Then we'll smear the stuff on and let him loose."

Molly, Hat, and I followed close behind. A short while later, we were at the edge of the clearing. We stopped behind the tall, thick shrubs and squatted down. We were completely hidden from view there.

Courtney and Denise had stepped into the clearing. They were standing in the tall grass, their arms crossed over their chests, their heads bowed as they discussed whatever it was they were discussing.

We could hear the murmur of their voices, but we weren't close enough to hear what they were saying. Behind them, we could hear the creek trickling past in its muddy bed.

"It's showtime, Buttercup," Charlene whispered, bending down to unleash the dog. She turned back to us. "As soon as he heads into the clearing, I'll start whistling."

Gripping the shaving cream can, I sprayed a thick puddle of white lather into my hand.

Suddenly I heard a sound behind us in the trees.

A rustling, crackling sound. Something running over the dry leaves and twigs. A squirrel appeared in a break between the shrubs.

Buttercup saw it, too. As I leaned over and reached out my hand to smear the shaving cream on his mouth, the big dog took off.

I toppled over onto my face.

I looked up in time to see the dog bolting for the trees, chasing after the squirrel.

My three friends were already on their feet. "Buttercup! Buttercup! Come back!" Charlene was shouting.

I climbed to my feet. I had shaving cream smeared over the front of my T-shirt. Ignoring it, I turned and ran into the trees after them.

They were already pretty far ahead of me. I couldn't see them. But I could hear Charlene yelling, "Buttercup! Come back! Buttercup — where *are* you?"

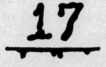

17

I ran as fast as I could and caught up with my friends. "Where — where's Buttercup?" I asked breathlessly.

"Over there somewhere, I think," Charlene replied, pointing to a thick clump of trees.

"No. I think I heard him over there," Hat said, pointing in the opposite direction.

"We can't lose him," I said, struggling to catch my breath. "He's too big to lose."

"I didn't know he could run that fast," Charlene said unhappily. "He really wants to catch that squirrel."

"Doesn't he know he has a job to do?" Molly asked, searching the trees.

"I — I shouldn't have let go of the leash," Charlene moaned. "Now we'll never catch the big oaf."

"Sure we will," I replied, trying to sound cheerful. "He'll come back to *us* after the squirrel runs away."

Dirt and dried leaves had stuck to the shaving cream when I fell over. Now I had a big, dark smear on my T-shirt. I wiped at it with my hand as my eyes searched the woods for Buttercup.

"We'd better split up," Charlene said. She looked really worried. "We've got to find him before he gets into some kind of trouble. He isn't used to the woods."

"Maybe he's by the creek," Molly suggested, straightening her glasses. She had a twig caught in her hair. I pulled it out for her.

"Let's stop talking and go find him," I urged impatiently. "Maybe we can still scare Courtney and Denise with him."

I'm always the optimist in the group.

"Let's just find him," Charlene murmured, a tight, worried expression on her face. "If anything happens to Buttercup . . ." She was too upset to finish her sentence.

We split up. I took the path that led toward the creek. I began jogging, pushing away low tree branches as I made my way along the twisting path. "Buttercup! Buttercup!" I called in a loud whisper.

How *could* that dumb dog mess us up like this? How could he be so irresponsible?

"Ow!" A sharp thorn tore through my wrist as I ran past a large bramble bush. I stopped to examine the cut, breathing hard. A small teardrop of bright red blood appeared on my wrist.

Ignoring it, I resumed my search. "Buttercup! Buttercup?"

I should be pretty near the creek by now, I realized. But I couldn't hear the sound of the water.

Was I on the right path? Had I gotten turned around somehow?

I began running faster, jumping over a fallen log, pushing my way through tall reeds. The ground became soft and marshy. My sneakers were sinking into soft mud as I ran.

Shouldn't the clearing be right up ahead?

Shouldn't the creek be on *this* side of the clearing?

I stopped. I leaned over, struggling to catch my breath, resting my hands on my knees.

When I looked up, I realized I was lost.

I gazed up to find the sun. Perhaps I could recapture my sense of direction. But the trees were too thick. Little sunlight filtered through.

"I'm lost," I said out loud, more startled than frightened. "I don't believe it. I'm lost in the woods."

I spun around, searching for something familiar. Slender, white-trunked trees nearly formed a thick fence behind me. Darker trees surrounded me on the three other sides.

"Hey — can anyone hear me?" I cried. My voice came out shrill and frightened.

"Can anyone *hear* me?" I repeated, forcing myself to shout louder.

No reply.

A bird cawed loudly overhead. I heard fluttering wings.

"Hey, Hat! Molly! Charlene!" I called their names several times.

No reply.

A cold shiver rolled down my back. "Hey, I'm lost!" I shouted. "Hey — somebody!"

And then I heard the crunch of footsteps to my left. Heavy footsteps. Coming toward me rapidly.

"Hey, guys — is that you?" I cried, listening hard.

No reply. The heavy footsteps moved closer.

I stared into the dark trees.

I heard the caw of another bird. More fluttering wings.

Heavy footsteps. Dry leaves crunching.

"Buttercup — is that you? Hey — Buttercup?"

It had to be the dog. I took a few steps toward the approaching sounds.

I stopped when the dog stepped into view.

"Buttercup?"

No.

I gasped as I stared into the glaring red eyes of another dog. An enormous, mean-looking dog, nearly as tall as a pony, with smooth, black fur.

It lowered its sleek head and snarled at me, its red eyes glowing angrily.

"Nice doggie," I said weakly. "Nice doggie."

It bared its teeth and let out a terrifying growl.

Then it took a running start and, snarling with fury, leapt at my throat.

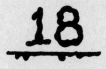

18

"Hey!" An alarmed voice called out from somewhere behind me.

The snarling dog appeared to stop in midair.

Its eyes still glowing like hot coals, it landed hard on all four legs.

"Hey — go away!" the voice cried.

I turned to see Hat running toward me, swinging a long stick in one hand. "Go away, dog!" Hat shouted.

The dog lowered its head and let out a growl, its eyes still on me. It took a reluctant step back, its smooth black tail tucked between its heavy legs. It took another step back. Then another.

"Go away!" I took up the cry. "Go away!"

I don't know if it was because there were now two of us, or whether it was the stick Hat was swinging in front of him — but the enormous creature suddenly turned and loped off into the trees.

"Oh, wow," I moaned. "Wow. Wow. That was close." I suddenly realized I'd been holding my breath for so long, my chest hurt. I let it out in a loud *whoosh*.

"Are you okay?" Hat asked.

"Yeah, I guess," I replied shakily. "Thanks for saving my life."

He stared into the trees where the dog had disappeared. "Was that a dog or a horse?" Hat cried. "He looked mean enough, didn't he?"

I nodded. My throat suddenly felt very dry. It was hard to talk. I knew I'd be seeing that growling beast again, in nightmares.

"Did you find Buttercup?" I managed to ask.

Hat kicked at a fallen tree trunk. He shook his head. "No. Not yet. Charlene's getting a little ballistic."

"I — I know how she feels," I stammered. I glanced to the trees. For some reason, I thought I saw the big, black dog coming back for me.

But it was just a gust of wind, shaking the leaves.

"We'd better get back," Hat said, giving the tree trunk a final kick.

I followed him along the path. It curved and then sloped downhill. Little creatures rustled the dry leaves at our feet. Chipmunks, I thought.

I didn't pay any attention to them. I was still picturing the enormous, growling monster, still thinking about my close call.

We caught up to Molly and Charlene a short while later. They both looked really miserable.

"What are we going to *do*?" Charlene whined. She had her hands jammed tightly into the pockets of her jeans. She looked about to cry. "I can't go home without Buttercup!" she wailed. "I can't!"

"I'll bet your dog went home," Molly said. "I'll bet that stupid dog is home already."

Charlene's face brightened a little. "Do you think so? You don't think he's lost in the woods?"

"Dogs don't get lost," I offered. "Only people get lost."

"He's right," Hat agreed. "Dogs have a great sense of direction. Buttercup is probably at home."

"Let's go check it out," Molly urged, putting a comforting hand on Charlene's shoulder.

"And what if he isn't there?" Charlene demanded miserably. "Then what?"

"Then we'll call the police and ask them to help us find him," Molly told her.

That answer seemed to satisfy Charlene. The four of us unhappily began trudging out of the woods.

We had just stepped out from the trees and were heading toward the street when Courtney and Denise came into view.

They were standing at the curb. There were two dogs standing with them.

Buttercup stood on one side of Courtney. The huge, black dog-monster sat on its haunches on Courtney's other side.

"Hi!" Courtney called as we went running up to them. "Do these dogs belong to any of you?"

I just stopped and stared in disbelief.

Buttercup was affectionately licking Courtney's hand. The big, black dog was tenderly licking her other hand.

"The Saint Bernard is mine!" Charlene cried happily.

"You should hold on to his leash," Courtney told her. "He was totally lost when I found him." She handed Buttercup's leash to Charlene.

Charlene thanked her.

"Isn't this other dog a sweetheart?" Courtney cooed. She bent down and gave the huge black monster a nose kiss.

That's when I decided to give up.

It was impossible, I saw. There was no way — *no way* — we would ever scare Courtney.

It was time to admit defeat, I told myself.

Little did I know just how scary things were soon going to get.

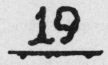

Icy hands, cold as death, wrapped around my neck.

I screamed.

Charlene laughed. "Eddie, what's your problem? A little tense?"

"Why are your hands so cold?" I demanded, rubbing my neck.

She held up a can of Coke. "I just took this from the fridge."

Everyone laughed at me.

The four of us were sitting in Charlene's den a few days later, trying to decide what to try next. It was about eight-thirty on a Thursday night. We'd told our parents we were studying together for our math final.

"I think we should just give up," I said glumly. "We can't scare Courtney. We just can't."

"Eddie's right," Hat agreed. He was sitting next to Molly on the brown leather couch. I was slouched in the big armchair across from them.

Charlene had dropped down to the shaggy white carpet.

"There's *got* to be a way," Charlene insisted. "Courtney isn't a robot, you know. She's *got* to get scared sometimes!"

"I'm not so sure," I said, shaking my head.

At that moment, Buttercup padded into the room, his tail wagging behind him. He made his way to Charlene and started licking her arm.

"Get that traitor out of here!" I demanded sharply.

Buttercup raised his head and gave me a long, wet stare with those sorrowful brown eyes of his.

"You heard me, Buttercup," I said coldly. "You're a traitor."

"He's just a dog," Charlene said, defending him. She pulled the furry beast down beside her on the rug.

"Dogs sure seem to like Courtney," Molly commented.

"Snakes and tarantulas like her, too," I added bitterly. "There's nothing Courtney is scared of. Nothing."

Molly suddenly got this devilish expression on her face. "Want to see something *really* scary?" she asked. She reached over to the other side of the couch and pulled the baseball cap off Hat's head.

"YUCK!" the three of us all cried at once. "Scary!"

Hat's dark hair was plastered to his head. It looked like wood or something. He had a deep red mark across his forehead made by the rim of the cap.

"Hey!" Hat cried angrily. He grabbed the cap back and jammed it onto his head.

"Don't you ever wash your hair?" Charlene cried.

"What for?" Hat replied. He got up and walked to the mirror so he could adjust the cap the way he liked it.

We talked about scaring Courtney for a while longer. We were pretty depressed about the whole thing. We just couldn't think of any good ideas.

At a little after nine o'clock, my mom called and told me I had to come home. So I said good night to my friends and headed out the door.

It had rained most of the day. Now the air was cool and wet. The front lawns shimmered wetly in the pale light from the street lamps.

My house was four blocks away on the same street. I wished I had ridden my bike. I don't really like walking alone this late at night. Some of the street lamps were out, and it was kind of creepy.

Okay, okay. I admit it. I'm a lot easier to scare than Courtney.

Cold hands on the back of my neck are enough to make me jump.

Maybe that's what we should try on Courtney, I thought as I crossed the street and started down the next block. Icy cold hands on the back of her neck . . .

I was passing an empty lot, a long rectangle of tall weeds and overgrown shrubs. In the corner of my eye, I saw something move along the ground.

A darting shadow, black against the yellow-gray ground.

Something scurrying through the tall weeds toward me.

I swallowed hard, feeling my throat tighten up. I started to jog.

The shadow slid toward me.

I heard a low moan.

Just the wind?

No. Too human to be the wind.

Another moan, more of a cry this time.

The trees all began to shake and whisper. Black shadows swept quickly toward me.

My heart pounding, I started to run. I crossed the street and kept running.

But the shadows were closing in. Darkening. About to sweep over me.

I knew I'd never make it home.

20

I was running as fast as I could. The dark hedges and trees flew by in a blur. My sneakers slapped the wet pavement loudly.

I could feel the blood pulsing at my temples as my house came into view. The yellow porchlight made the front lawn glisten brightly.

Almost there, I thought. Almost there. *Please* let me make it inside.

A few seconds later, I was lurching up the driveway. I darted past the front walk, along the side of the house, and up to the kitchen door.

With a final, desperate burst of energy, I pushed open the door with my shoulder, bolted into the kitchen, slammed the door behind me, and locked it.

Gasping for breath, my chest heaving up and down, my throat dry and aching, I stood there for a long while, leaning my back against the door, struggling to catch my breath.

It didn't take me long to realize that no one had really been chasing me. I knew it was all my imagination.

This had happened to me before.

Lots of times.

Why am I such a scaredy-cat? I asked myself, starting to feel a little more normal now that I was home safe and sound.

And, then, standing in the empty kitchen, waiting for my heart to stop pounding, I realized what my friends and I had been doing wrong. I realized why we hadn't been able to scare Courtney.

"Eddie, is that you?" my mom called from the living room.

"Yeah. I'm home," I called back. I hurried through the hall and poked my head into the living room. "I just have to make one call," I told her.

"But you just got home — " Mom started to protest.

I was already halfway up the stairs. "Just one call!" I shouted down.

I flew into my room, grabbed the phone, and called Charlene. She picked up after the second ring. "Hello?"

"We've been doing it all wrong!" I told her breathlessly.

"Eddie? Are you home already? Did you run all the way?"

"We've been doing it all wrong," I repeated,

ignoring her questions. "We've got to scare Courtney at night! At *night*! Not in the daytime. Everything is scarier at night!"

There was a brief silence. Charlene must have
been thinking about what I was saying. Finally,
she said, "You're right, Eddie. Everything *is* a
lot scarier at night. But we still don't have any
good ideas."

"Yeah, you're right," I admitted.

"We can't just jump out at Courtney in the dark
and yell 'Boo!' " Charlene said.

Charlene was right. Nighttime was definitely
the right time to scare Courtney. But we needed
an idea. A really good, terrifying idea.

Strangely enough, Courtney gave me the idea
herself the next morning.

21

We were discussing monsters at morning meeting.

We have morning meeting to start each day. We all gather in the meeting area at one end of the classroom. Mr. Melvin leans against the chalkboard or sits on a little three-legged stool he keeps there. And we discuss all kinds of things.

Actually, the same three or four kids have the discussion. The rest of us just sit there and pretend to listen while we struggle to wake up.

Of course Courtney is one of the big talkers. She's always bright and enthusiastic, even first thing in the morning. And she's never afraid to give her opinion on *anything*.

Today, Mr. Melvin was telling us how people have always believed in monsters, since very early times. "People have a need to create monsters," he said. "It helps us believe that the real world isn't quite as scary. The real world isn't as scary as the monsters we can dream up."

He went on like that for quite a while. I don't think anyone was really listening. It was very early in the morning, after all.

"There are countless legends and myths, stories and movies about monsters," Mr. Melvin was saying. "But no one has ever proven that monsters exist. Mainly because they exist only in our imaginations."

"That's not true," Courtney interrupted. She always started talking without raising her hand first. She never cared if she was interrupting someone or not.

Mr. Melvin's bushy black eyebrows shot up on his shiny forehead. "Do *you* have proof that monsters exist, Courtney?" he asked.

"Courtney's a monster," someone whispered behind me. I heard a few kids snicker.

I was sitting on the window ledge. The morning sunlight through the window felt warm against my back. Molly was beside me, trying to unstick some gum from her braces.

"My uncle is a scientist," Courtney said. "He told me that the Loch Ness Monster in Scotland really exists. It lives in this big lake, and it looks like a sea serpent. And people have taken pictures of it."

"Those pictures aren't really proof — " Mr. Melvin started.

But Courtney kept going. She never stopped until she'd said all she had to say. "My uncle says that Bigfoot is real, too. He's seen photos of Bigfoot's footprints, taken in the Himalaya Mountains."

There were whispered comments around the room. I glanced at Hat, who was sitting on the floor in the middle of the meeting area, and he rolled his eyes at me.

"People don't just imagine all the monsters," Courtney concluded. "They're real. A lot of people are just too scared to admit that they're real."

"That's a very interesting theory," Mr. Melvin said, scratching his neck. "Does anyone agree with Courtney? How many of you believe in monsters?"

A few kids raised their hands. I didn't notice how many. I was lost in my own thoughts.

Courtney believes in monsters, I told myself. She really believes that monsters exist.

Slowly, an idea began to hatch in my mind.

Monsters . . . monsters . . .

Monsters at night. In the dark . . .

Thanks to Courtney, I was beginning to get the perfect plan for scaring her. The perfect plan that *had* to work!

22

I asked Kevin to help me, and he refused. So I brought Hat, Molly, and Charlene over to beg him.

"Let me get this straight," Kevin said, frowning at us. "You want me and two friends to get into our Mud Monster costumes and scare some girl in the woods?"

"Not *some girl*," I told him impatiently. "Courtney."

"She deserves to be scared," Charlene quickly added. "Really. She's been asking for it."

It was Saturday afternoon. We were standing in my back yard. Kevin had the garden hose in his hand. He did a lot of lawn chores on Saturdays. He was about to water the flower beds.

"The video is all finished," Kevin said, tightening the nozzle. "I'm glad I don't have to get into that costume and put on all that drippy makeup again."

"Please!" I begged.

"It'll be fun," Hat told Kevin. "It'll be really funny."

Kevin turned the nozzle, but no water came out.

"The hose is tangled," I said, pointing. "Let me untangle it for you." I bent down and started to work the knot out of the hose.

"Courtney and her friend Denise have this tree house in the woods by Muddy Creek," Charlene told Kevin.

"I know," Kevin replied. "We did our video there. We used the tree house in the video. The Mud Monsters climbed up into the tree house to murder a guy. It was cool."

"Great!" Molly cried. "How about an instant replay?"

"Please!" I pleaded. I'd been doing a *lot* of pleading with Kevin ever since I got the idea.

"So you want the three of us to wait in the woods at night, right?" Kevin asked.

I untangled the hose. Water sprayed out onto Hat's sneakers.

He jumped back with a startled cry. We all laughed.

"Sorry," Kevin said, turning the spray on the flowers. "It was an accident."

"Yeah. You and your friends wait in the woods. Then, when it's really dark, you come out and scare Courtney to death!"

"You mean we make weird sounds and stagger around with slimy mud dripping off us and pretend to chase her," Kevin said.

"Right," I replied eagerly. I could see he was starting to get interested.

"How are you going to get her to the tree house at night?" Kevin asked.

A good question. I hadn't really thought about that.

"I'll get her there," Molly said suddenly. She'd been very quiet all afternoon.

"You'll pretend to be Denise?" I asked. "That didn't work out well last time."

"I won't need to be Denise this time," Molly said mysteriously. "Don't worry. I'll get her there."

Kevin raised the hose till the strong spray rose up the side of the house. He had his back turned to me. I couldn't tell what he was thinking.

"Well? Will you do it?" I asked, ready to start pleading and begging again. "Will you get your friends to help out, too?"

"What's in it for me?" Kevin asked without turning around.

"Uh . . ." I thought quickly. "I'll be your servant for a week, Kevin," I said. "I'll do all your lawn chores. I'll mow the lawn. I'll water and weed. And . . . I'll do the dishes every night. And I'll clean your room."

He turned and narrowed his eyes at me. "Get serious," he muttered.

"No. Really!" I insisted. "I'll be a total servant. Total! For a whole week."

He turned off the nozzle. The water fizzled, then slowed to a drip. "How about for a month?" he said.

Whoa. A month was a long time. A month of doing all of Kevin's chores and jumping at his every command. A whole month . . .

Was it worth it? Was it worth turning myself into a pitiful, overworked servant for a month just to scare Courtney?

Of *course* it was!

"Okay," I said. "A month."

He grinned and shook my hand. His hand was wet from the hose.

He handed the hose to me. "Take over, servant," he ordered.

I took the hose from him. Water dripped onto the front of my jeans.

"When do you want the three Mud Monsters to appear?" Kevin asked. "When do you want to scare Courtney?"

"Tomorrow night," I replied.

23

I'm not really sure how the legend of the Mud Monsters got started. I heard about them first from another kid when I was little. The kid was trying to scare me, and he did a pretty good job of it.

The legend goes something like this:

Some early settlers of our town were too poor to build houses. So they set up little huts in the woods along the banks of Muddy Creek.

The creek was much bigger then, much deeper and wider. It wasn't just a muddy trickle of water the way it is today.

The people were poor and hard-working and, pretty soon, they'd built an entire village of huts along the creek. But the people in town looked down on them. They refused to help them in any way.

The town officials refused to share the city water supply with the Muddy Creek people. The store owners refused to let them buy anything on credit.

Many of the Creek people were going hungry. Many of them were sick. But the town refused to help.

This all happened over a hundred years ago. Maybe even longer.

One night, there was a terrible rainstorm. Pouring rains and hurricane winds.

Before the Creek people could run to safety, the creek rose up. The muddy banks towered up like a tidal wave, a tidal wave of heavy, black mud.

The mud swept over the village. It buried all the huts and all the people. Like lava from a volcano, it buried everything beneath it.

The next morning, there was nothing left of the village. The creek rolled by, high on its muddy banks. The woods were silent and empty.

The village and all the people were gone.

Only not completely.

According to the legend, once a year when the moon is full, the villagers rise up from the mud. They're monsters now, half-dead and half-alive. They're Mud Monsters.

And once a year the Mud Monsters pull themselves up from their muddy graves to dance in the moonlight — and to seek revenge on the townspeople who refused to help them.

That's the local legend, as much as I know of it.

Of course it isn't true. But it's a really good story, I think. And it's been told again and again, passed on from one generation to the next.

The story has scared an awful lot of kids. Including me.

And now, on Sunday night, Kevin and his two fellow Mud Monsters were about to terrify Courtney, the girl who couldn't be terrified.

At a little after seven, Kevin was in the bathroom, putting the finishing touches on his costume. He had thick, brownish-orange mud caked over his face and hair. He wore a loose-fitting black shirt over baggy black jeans. His clothing was dripping with mud, too.

I stepped into the doorway and examined him as he piled more thick goo onto his hair. "Yuck. You really look gross," I told him.

"Thanks, punk," he replied. "Did you finish loading the dishwasher?"

"Yes," I said grudgingly.

"And did you collect all my dirty clothes from my room and put them in the hamper?"

"Yes," I muttered.

"Yes, *sir*," he corrected me. "A servant should always be polite."

"Yes, *sir*," I repeated. He had been running me ragged ever since I'd agreed to be his servant. It was truly unbelievable how many chores he found for me to do!

But now the big moment was rapidly approaching, the moment that would make my month of drudgery worthwhile.

Kevin turned to me. "How do I look?"

"Like a pile of mud," I replied.

He smiled. "Thanks." I followed him down to the front hall. He picked up the car keys from the little table. "I'm going to drive over and pick up my two friends," he said, admiring his gruesome appearance in the hall mirror. "Then we'll find hiding places in the woods. Want a lift?"

I shook my head. "No. Thanks. I've got to go to Molly's first. There's one little detail we have to take care of."

"What's that?" Kevin asked.

"Getting Courtney to the woods," I replied.

24

"Hi, Eddie. What's going on?" Molly's dad asked.

We were standing in Molly's kitchen. Her dad pulled open the refrigerator and removed a can of ginger ale. Then he searched the shelves, squinting into the light.

"Nothing much, Dad," Molly replied nervously. "Eddie and I are just hanging out."

He turned away from the refrigerator. "You two want to play some Scrabble or something?"

"No. No thanks," Molly replied quickly. "Not tonight, okay?"

I glanced up at the kitchen clock. It was getting late. We didn't have time for any long discussions with Molly's dad. We had to get Courtney to the woods.

"How about some card games?" her dad said, sticking his head back in the refrigerator. "You've been wanting me to teach you poker. I don't have much to do tonight, so — "

"Eddie and I have to talk about stuff," Molly said. "And . . . uh . . . we have to call some kids."

Her dad looked hurt. He pulled some cold cuts from the fridge and started to make a sandwich. "You two hungry?"

"No. We're not," Molly replied impatiently. She pulled me toward the den.

"Molly, we've got to hurry," I whispered.

"Tell me about it," Molly said dryly. She pushed her glasses up on her nose. "Here. You can listen on this phone, Eddie. I'll go upstairs and call Courtney."

"What are you going to say? You're not going to pretend to be Denise?" I was starting to feel really nervous. We should have called Courtney a lot earlier. We shouldn't have waited until the last minute.

Molly flashed me a mysterious smile. "You'll see," she said slyly. Then she disappeared upstairs.

I paced back and forth in the den for a minute or so, giving Molly time enough to dial. Then I carefully picked up the receiver and held it to my ear.

Molly already had Courtney on the phone. "Who is this?" Courtney was asking.

"It's Molly," was the reply.

I held my breath. Why was Molly telling Courtney the truth?

"Hi, Molly. What's up?" Courtney asked, surprise in her voice. She and Molly had never exactly been pals.

"I heard something I thought you'd be interested in," Molly said breathlessly. "I just heard that the Mud Monsters are supposed to appear at the creek tonight."

There was a long silence on Courtney's end. Finally, she said, "This is a joke, right?"

"No," Molly answered quickly. "I really heard it. They said it's a full moon, and this is the night the Mud Monsters rise up every year."

"Molly, give me a break," Courtney said sarcastically. "Come on. Why'd you call me?"

She isn't buying it, I thought, gripping the phone tightly, too nervous to breathe. Courtney isn't buying it. Molly's idea is a flop.

"Well, Courtney, you said in school that you believed in monsters," Molly said. "And so when I heard about the Mud Monsters, I thought you would be really desperate to see them."

"Where did you hear about this?" Courtney demanded suspiciously.

"On the radio," Molly lied. "I just heard it on the radio. They said the Mud Monsters were going to rise up in the woods tonight when the moon is up."

"Well, *you* go," Courtney said coldly. "You can tell me about it in school on Monday."

Oh, no, I thought. Failure. Total failure. The

whole plan is a bust. My brother is going to kill me!

"Well, I might go," Molly told Courtney, not giving up. "I mean, you don't get a chance to see real monsters very often. But if you're scared, Courtney, you should stay home."

"Huh? What did you just say?" Courtney demanded, her voice rising shrilly.

"I said," Molly repeated, "if you're too scared, you definitely should stay away from the woods."

"Me? Scared?" Courtney's voice was almost high enough for only dogs to hear. "I'm not scared of any Mud Monsters, Molly. I'll see you there in ten minutes. Unless *you're* too scared."

"No. Really. Stay home," Molly told Courtney. "I don't want to be responsible. If you start to panic and you get hurt — "

"See you there," Courtney said sharply. She hung up.

A few seconds later, Molly returned to the den with a wide, pleased smile on her face. "Am I a genius, or what?" she asked.

"You're a genius," I replied. "Let's get going."

25

I felt a cold shiver as Molly and I neared the woods at Muddy Creek. The air was surprisingly cool and damp. Slender wisps of black clouds floated over the full moon, which still hovered low over the trees.

"This is exciting," Molly said, her eyes searching the dark trees ahead of us. "I can't believe we're finally going to scare Courtney."

"I can't believe it, either," I said. "I just keep wondering what will go wrong *this* time."

"Nothing will go wrong," Molly assured me. "Stop being such a pessimist. Tonight's the night, Eddie."

Charlene and Hat were waiting for us at the edge of the woods. Molly saw them first and waved. We both began jogging over to them.

"Have you seen my brother and his two friends?" I asked, gazing toward the dark woods.

"No," Hat replied.

"But we saw Courtney," Charlene reported.

"She and Denise were hurrying to the tree house."

"She brought Denise?" I cried. "Great! We'll terrify Denise, too!"

"Did they see you?" Molly asked Charlene.

"No way," Charlene replied. "Hat and I hid. Over there." She pointed to a cluster of thick shrubs.

The woods suddenly grew brighter. I glanced up to see that the wispy clouds had rolled away from the moon. Pale yellow light, eerie light, washed over us.

The trees suddenly shook in a gust of wind. It sounded like whispering all around us.

"My brother and his friends must be hiding down by the creek," I said. "Come on. Let's go. We don't want to miss the big moment."

The four of us made our way through the trees. We tried to walk silently, but twigs and dried leaves crackled noisily under our sneakers.

I gasped when I heard a soft moan.

A haunting, sad cry. Mournful.

I stopped and listened. Another moan.

"Wh-what's that?" I stammered in a choked whisper.

"Sounds like a bird. A dove, maybe," Charlene replied.

Another moan. Yes. It was a dove, up in a tree.

"Hey, Eddie, you're not freaking *already*, are you?" Hat demanded. He slapped me hard on the back. "You've got to keep it together, man."

"I'm together," I muttered. I felt embarrassed that I'd panicked over a stupid dove. I was glad it was too dark for them to see me blushing.

I reached out and flipped Hat's cap around, just to get my mind off the dove.

"Hey!" Hat cried out, spinning around angrily.

"Ssshhh. Quiet. Courtney and Denise will hear us," Molly scolded.

We made our way quickly toward the tree house. The woods grew darker as we crept under the whispering trees. We huddled closer together as we walked. No one whispered or spoke.

I heard more low moans. Soft cries.

I forced myself to ignore them. I wasn't going to allow myself to be frightened by any more birds.

It seemed as if we had walked for hours, but I knew it had only been a couple of minutes. My throat felt dry, and my knees were a little shaky. Just from the excitement, I guessed.

"Oh!" I cried out as I tripped over something, a raised tree root or a rock. I went sprawling in the dirt face first. "Ow."

Hat and Charlene pulled me up quickly. "Are you okay?" Charlene whispered.

"Yeah. Fine," I muttered, brushing myself off. I had landed hard on my right elbow, and it was throbbing like crazy.

"Stop trying to scare us," Charlene scolded me.

"I'm not," I protested. Rubbing my aching elbow, I followed them along the path.

We stopped at the edge of the clearing. Keeping in the darkness of the trees, we stared out at the tree house.

It was more like a platform with walls than a house. I mean, it didn't have a roof or anything. Courtney and Denise were perched in it, leaning against one side.

Moonlight washed over the clearing, and I could see them both clearly. Courtney had a pair of binoculars up to her eyes. Denise was shining a flashlight into the trees. She had a camera around her neck.

Perfect, I thought, snickering to myself. They always have to be the perfect scientists. I was surprised they hadn't made work sheets so they could check off the Mud Monsters when they saw them. Under wildlife!

My three friends and I squatted down behind a clump of tall weeds and watched them. Courtney and Denise kept chatting as they peered out over the tree house wall. But I couldn't hear what they were saying.

"I can't wait!" Hat whispered, leaning toward me. His dark eyes flashed excitedly under the brim of his cap. He was furiously chewing a big wad of gum. "Where's your brother?" he asked.

My eyes searched the trees that lined the creek bed just behind the clearing. "I don't see him," I whispered to Hat. "But he and his friends are there somewhere. And they're going to come walking out any minute."

"And then the fun will begin," Hat whispered, grinning.

"Yeah," I agreed. "Then the fun will begin."

But I had this gnawing doubt, a heavy feeling of dread.

Where *were* Kevin and his friends?

Where were they?

And then I saw something moving behind the tree house at the edge of the clearing.

26

I grabbed Hat's sleeve when I saw the moving shadows near the trees. "Look!" I whispered, my heart pounding. I pointed across the clearing.

But I didn't need to point. He saw them, too. We all saw them.

Courtney and Denise were facing the other direction, unaware that something was happening behind them.

I stared hard, holding my breath, keeping low behind the weeds.

I saw a dark figure moving slowly toward the tree house.

Then I saw another figure behind it. It seemed to be pulling itself up from the mud.

A third figure staggered into the light.

Yes!

The three Mud Monsters!

Kevin and his friends had come through for us!

Courtney and Denise still didn't see them.

Courtney was leaning on the tree house wall, peering through the binoculars.

Denise was aiming the flashlight in the other direction.

I could see Kevin and his friends clearly now. They looked great!

Their heads were covered with wet, dark mud. Their clothes appeared tattered and decayed.

Dripping mud, they staggered forward, like zombies, with their arms outstretched.

Closer. Closer to the tree house.

Turn around! I silently urged Courtney and Denise.

Turn around — and start screaming your heads off!

But Courtney and Denise still didn't turn around. They still had no idea the three gruesome Mud Monsters were sneaking up behind them.

I turned and glanced quickly at my three friends. Molly and Charlene were frozen like statues, their mouths wide open, their eyes bulging, enjoying the show. Hat stared without blinking. Watching gleefully. Waiting.

We were all waiting for our two victims to realize the Mud Monsters were approaching.

Suddenly, as I stared at the three staggering Mud Monsters in the clearing, I heard a rustling sound behind me.

Crackling twigs. The scrape of shoes against the ground.

Footsteps.

Low murmuring voices.

"Huh?" With a gasp of surprise, I turned back.

And saw three *other* Mud Monsters standing behind us!

"No!" I tried to scream, but my voice came out a choked whisper.

Hat, Molly, and Charlene spun around as the three new Mud Monsters moved closer.

And I recognized Kevin in the middle of them.

"K-Kevin!" I stammered.

"Sorry, punk," Kevin whispered. "But we had a flat tire."

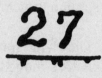

27

"Are we too late?" Kevin asked.

I didn't reply. I couldn't.

I turned back to the clearing. The three Mud Monsters were staggering right behind the tree house. Their sunken eyes peered out from the wet mud that dripped down their faces.

And then I saw more of them. I saw arms poking up from the dirt. I saw mud-covered heads appear. More and more bodies rose up silently from the marshy ground.

Dark figures, dripping with thick mud, pushed themselves up and began staggering across the clearing. Their bare feet slapped the mud as they walked.

There were dozens of them now. Skinny, scraggly, twisted, mud-drenched bodies, all lurching toward the tree house. Dozens. And dozens more, pulling themselves up from under the ground.

"Run!" I screamed, jumping out from behind

the weeds. "Courtney! Denise! Run! *Run!*"

They hesitated. Then they finally saw the hideous monsters.

Courtney's shrill scream rang out through the trees.

She screamed out in terror. Again. And then again.

She and Denise were both screaming.

It should have been our big moment, our triumph.

But it wasn't.

The two girls screamed in shrill horror.

And then I realized we were *all* screaming.

Their feet smacking wetly over the ground, the Mud Monsters staggered forward.

I saw Courtney and Denise leap to the ground.

And then I saw them running, screaming in terror as they ran.

And then I was running, too. Running through the dark trees. Running from the woods.

Running. Running. Running from the mud-covered monsters I knew I'd never forget, no matter how far I ran.

Well, that all happened two weeks ago. Two long weeks ago.

The horror is over. It's all behind us.

But I still don't go out much. I really don't like to leave the house.

Neither do my friends.

Yesterday, Kevin asked me if I wanted to see his Mud Monsters video. It's all edited and finished, he said.

I told him no thanks. I really don't want to watch it.

I've been very nervous and tense since that night in the woods.

My friends have been nervous and tense, too. We're all totally stressed out.

Except for Courtney.

You know what Courtney has been doing? She's been bragging to everyone that she was right. That there really *are* monsters in the world.

Courtney's been bragging to everyone how she proved there are real monsters because she saw them.

She's worse than ever.

My friends and I, we'd really like to give Courtney a good scare.

We'd really like to scare Courtney once and for all.

But we can't. We're just too scared.

Add *more*

Goosebumps

to your collection . . .
A chilling preview of
what's next from
R.L. STINE

ONE DAY AT HORRORLAND

2

"I can't believe someone would build a big theme park out in the wilderness," Dad declared.

We were driving through what seemed like an endless forest. Tall, old trees leaned over the two-lane road, nearly blocking out the late morning sun.

"Maybe they haven't built the park yet," Mom suggested. "Maybe they're going to clear out these trees and build the park here."

All three of us in the back seat were hoping Mom was wrong. And she was.

The road curved sharply. And as we came out of the curve, we saw the tall gates to the park straight up ahead.

Behind a tall, purple fence, HorrorLand seemed to stretch for miles. Leaning forward in my seat, I could see the tops of rides and strange, colorful buildings. As we drove across the enormous parking lot, eerie chords of organ music invaded the car.

"YAAAAAY! This looks *great!*" Luke exclaimed.

Clay and I enthusiastically agreed. I couldn't wait to get out of the car and see everything.

"The parking lot is nearly empty," Dad said, glancing uneasily at Mom.

"That means we won't have to wait in long lines!" I quickly exclaimed.

"I think Lizzy is excited about this place," Mom commented, smiling.

"Me, too!" Luke cried. He punched Clay enthusiastically on the shoulder. Luke always has to be punching or pinching somebody.

We crossed the wide parking lot. I saw a few cars parked near the front gate. At the far side of the lot stood a row of purple-and-green buses with the word *HorrorLand* across the side.

As we rode closer, I got a good look at the front gate. The same monster we had seen behind the billboard rose up behind a big purple-and-green sign over the gate. The sign read: *THE HORRORLAND HORRORS WELCOME YOU TO HORRORLAND!*

"I don't *get* that sign," Mom said. "What are the HorrorLand Horrors?"

"We'll find out!" I exclaimed happily.

The solemn, eerie organ music floated heavily over the parking lot. Dad pulled into a space in an empty aisle to the right of the front gate.

Luke and I pushed open the back doors before the car had even stopped. "Let's go!" I cried.

Luke, Clay, and I started trotting toward the gate. As I ran, I stared up at the green monster over the sign. This one didn't move its head like the billboard monster. But it looked very real.

I glanced back and saw that Mom and Dad were hurrying to catch up with us. "This is going to be way cool!" I exclaimed.

And then I gasped as a deafening explosion made the ground shake.

And I stared back in horror as our car burst apart, exploding into a million pieces.

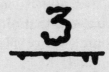

3

It took me a long while to stop screaming. Finally, I swallowed hard, choking back my cries.

We all stared in shock. Small chunks of twisted metal and a few burning cinders were all that was left of our car.

"How — ?" was all Dad managed to say.

"I — I d-don't believe it!" I stammered.

"Thank goodness we were all out of the car!" Mom cried. She gathered us up in a big hug. "Thank goodness we're all okay."

Luke and Clay still hadn't uttered a sound. They stood wide-eyed, staring at the spot where the car had stood.

"My car!" Dad choked out in a horrified whisper. "My car . . . How? How?"

"We're safe," Mom murmured. "We're all safe. What a terrifying explosion. I can't get the sound of it out of my ears."

"I — I've got to call the police!" Dad sputtered.

He began trotting to the gate, shaking his head, muttering to himself.

"How could the car just blow up like that, dear?" Mom asked, hurrying after him. "What would make it *do* that?"

"How should I know?" Dad snapped angrily. "I — I don't get it! I really don't! And *now* what are we going to do?" He sounded really panicked.

I didn't blame him. The explosion was really scary.

And when I realized that we could have all been inside the car when it went off, I had cold chills down my back.

"Maybe there's a rental car place we can call," Mom suggested.

Mom is like me, calm in any emergency.

We followed Dad as he went running up to the ticket booth at the entrance. A green monster stood in the booth. He had bulging yellow eyes, and dark horns curled over his head. It was a really great costume.

"Welcome to HorrorLand," he said in a gruff, low voice. A loud stab of organ music rose up from inside the ticket booth. "I am a HorrorLand Horror. All of the Horrors and I hope you have a scary day."

"My car!" Dad cried frantically. "There was an explosion. I need a phone!"

"I'm sorry, sir. No phones," the guy in the monster costume replied.

"Huh?" Dad's face was bright red again. His forehead was drenched with sweat. "But I *need* a phone! Right away!" Dad insisted, glaring angrily at the green monster. "My car exploded! We're stuck here!"

"We'll take care of you," the Horror replied, lowering his gruff voice nearly to a whisper.

"You'll *what*?" Dad cried. "We need a car. I need to get to a phone! Don't you understand?"

"No phones," the monster repeated. "But, please, sir. Allow us to take care of you. I promise we will take care of everything. Don't let this spoil your visit to HorrorLand."

"Spoil my visit?!" Dad shrieked, his face growing even redder. "But my car — !"

Another loud stab of organ music made me jump. The creepy music made me feel as if I were actually in a horror movie!

"We will take care of you. I promise," the Horror said. A strange smile crossed his face. His yellow eyes lit up. "Please enjoy your stay, and do not worry about transportation. The other Horrors and I will see that you are properly taken care of."

"But — but — " Dad sputtered.

The Horror gestured toward the park. "Please enter as our guests. Free admission. I apologize for your car. But, please, do not worry. I promise you will have no need to worry about your car."

Dad turned back to us, sweat dripping down

his forehead. I could see that he was really upset. "I — I can't enjoy an amusement park now," he said. "I can't believe this happened. I really can't. We've got to get a car somehow, and — "

"Oh, please, Dad!" Luke cried. "Please! Can't we go inside? He said he'll take care of it for us."

"Just for a little while?" I joined my brother in pleading.

"We've had such a long drive," Mom told Dad. "Let's go in for a short while. Let them blow off some steam."

Dad thought about it, frowning hard. "Okay. Just for a little while," he agreed finally.

The organ music grew louder as we stepped through the gate. "Wow! Look at this place!" I cried. "It really is like being in a horror movie."

We were standing on a brown, cobbled street. Strange, dark cottages tilted up on both sides of the street. Tall trees along the street nearly blocked out all the sunlight. The air carried a chill.

Low howls, like wolf howls, floated out from the cottages.

"Cool!" Luke declared.

A sign proclaimed: *WELCOME TO WERE-WOLF VILLAGE. DO NOT FEED THE WERE-WOLVES. IF YOU CAN HELP IT.*

The frightening howls grew louder.

Luke and I laughed at the sign.

I saw a green monster, one of the Horrors, staring out at us through a dark window in the cottage across the narrow street. Another Horror walked past carrying a very real-looking human head. He grasped it by its long, blond hair and bounced it up and down, sort of like a yo-yo, as he walked.

"Cool!" Luke proclaimed again. It seemed to be his word of the day.

We walked along the cobbled street. The sound of our thudding sneakers echoed off the cottage walls.

"Ohh!" We all let out cries of surprise as a long, low, gray wolf ran in front of us. It disappeared around the side of a cottage before we really got a good look at it.

"Was that a real wolf?" Clay asked, his voice shaking.

"Of course not," I told him. "It was probably a dog. Or else it was mechanical."

"Well, they certainly keep this park clean," Mom said, trying to sound cheerful. "There isn't a piece of trash or dirt anywhere. Of course, it isn't very crowded."

Dad lingered behind. "I — I've got to find a phone," he said fretfully. "I can't enjoy this until I know we have a way to get home."

"But, dear — " Mom started.

"There's got to be a phone somewhere," Dad interrupted. "Go on without me."

"No. I'll come with you," Mom said. "You're in such a frantic state. You'll need me to make the calls for you. The kids will have a better time without us hanging around anyway."

"Leave them?" Dad cried. "You mean, let them go on their own?"

"Of course," Mom said, hurrying back to him. "They'll be perfectly fine. This looks like a very nice place. What could happen?"

What could happen?

With those words, Mom and Dad rushed off to find a phone.

"Meet back here!" Mom called to us.

Luke, Clay, and I were suddenly on our own.

I turned to watch Mom and Dad hurry away.

I turned back in time to see a gray wolf edging out from behind the cottage. It lowered its head and let out a rumbling warning growl.

All three of us froze as we realized its hungry red eyes were locked on us.

4

I cried out and pulled Luke and Clay back.

The wolf slithered out, holding its head low, glaring up at us with wide red eyes, its mouth open hungrily.

"It — it's real!" Clay declared, swallowing hard. I had my hand on his shoulder. I could feel him trembling.

The wolf let out a low growl.

Then it slid back behind the cottage wall.

"I think it's some kind of robot or something," I told Clay.

"Let's go somewhere else," Clay replied, suddenly very pale.

"What does that sign up there say?" Luke asked. He went running over the dark cobblestones to the sign, and Clay and I followed.

The sign read: *NO PINCHING.*

Luke laughed. "That's stupid."

"What a dumb sign!" Clay agreed.

"That sign was meant just for you, Luke!" I

exclaimed. I gave him a hard pinch on the arm.

"Hey! Can't you read?" he shouted angrily, pointing to the sign.

I saw a green Horror watching us from down the street. Then I saw a family making its way behind the row of cottages. There was a mother, a father, and a little girl. The little girl was crying, for some reason. The parents had their hands on her shoulders and looked very upset.

A wolf howl cut through the air.

"Let's find some rides!" Clay suggested.

"Some *scary* rides!" Luke added.

Walking side by side, keeping close together, we made our way out of the Werewolf Village. The street widened into a round plaza. Bright sunlight returned as soon as we stepped out of the village.

Several purple-and-green buildings surrounded the plaza. I saw a few more families and several green-costumed Horrors keeping an eye on everything. A pudgy Horror behind a green-and-purple cart was selling ice cream cones — *black* ice cream!

"Yuck!" Luke declared, making a face.

We hurried past the cart, past another *No Pinching* sign, and stopped in front of what appeared to be a tall purple mountain.

"It's a ride!" I told them.

A doorway was cut into the side of the mountain. And above the doorway was a sign: *DOOM*

SLIDE. WILL YOU BE THE ONE TO SLIDE FOREVER?

"Cool!" Luke cried, slapping Clay a high five.

"I'll bet you climb to the top, then slide all the way down," I said, pointing to the top of the mountain-shaped building.

"Let's go!" Luke cried excitedly.

We ran to the building, then through the open doorway in its side. It was dark and cold inside. A wide ramp curved up toward the top.

I could hear kids squealing and laughing, but I couldn't see them. The three of us half-walked, half-ran up the ramp, eager to get to the top.

About halfway up, we stopped to read another sign: WARNING! — YOU MAY BE THE ONE TO SLIDE TO YOUR DOOM!

Now I could hear kids screaming as they slid down. But it was too dark to see anything. "Are you scared, Clay?" I asked, noticing his tight expression.

"No way!" he insisted, embarrassed by my question. "I've seen these things before. They're like really huge sliding boards. You just sit on them and slide down."

"Hurry!" Luke shouted, running ahead of us.

"Hey — wait up!" I called. I followed them to the top of the ramp. We found ourselves on a wide platform. A row of long, curving sliding boards stretched to the end of the platform. The sliding boards were numbered from one to ten.

In the dim light, I saw two Horrors watching us approach. They stood in front of the sliding boards. Their bulging yellow eyes lit up as we hurried over to them.

"Do you slide all the way down?" Luke asked one of them.

The Horror nodded.

"Do you go really fast?" Clay asked, lingering a few feet behind us.

The Horror nodded again. "It's a long way down," he rumbled.

"Be careful which slide you pick," the other Horror warned. "Don't pick the Doom Slide." He gestured to the number painted in black in front of each slide.

"Yes. Don't pick the Doom Slide," his partner repeated. "You'll slide down forever and ever."

I laughed.

He was just trying to scare us — *wasn't* he?

About the Author

R.L. STINE is the author of over two dozen best-selling thrillers and mysteries for young people. Recent titles for teenagers include *The Hitch-hiker, Halloween Night, The Dead Girlfriend*, and *The Baby-sitter III*, all published by Scholastic. He is also the author of the *Fear Street* series.

When he isn't writing scary books, he is head writer of the children's TV show *Eureeka's Castle*, seen on Nickelodeon.

Bob lives in New York City with his wife, Jane, and thirteen-year-old son, Matt.

GET
Goosebumps
by R.L. Stine

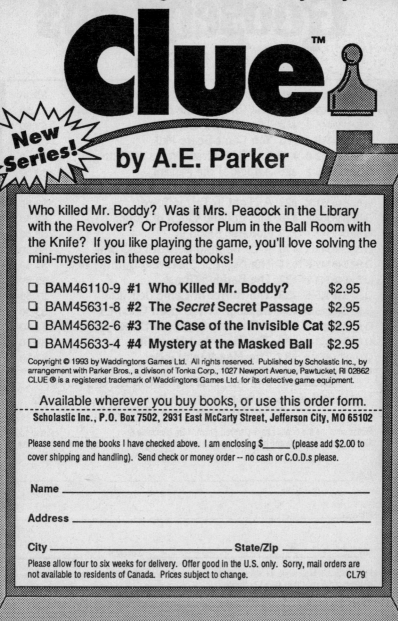